DEDICATION

For my readers! You are my rock stars! Thank you.

PROLOGUE

"Name your price."

Chance Valentine slowly looked up and met the bright blue stare of the man seated across from him.

"You know I can pay it," Will Hawthorne said, leaning forward. "So let's cut through the bullshit and get this job done."

Chance kept his face expressionless. "You have your own security team. I really don't see why you need me anymore." Will Hawthorne was one wealthy bastard — with bastard being the keyword. The man had enemies that stretched for miles, rivals that he'd stepped on — no *stomped on* — as he climbed to the top of the business world. The guy was also Chance's ex-boss.

"She doesn't trust anyone else on the team. She ditches the guards as fast as I put them on her."

Her.

It got a little harder for Chance to keep that expressionless mask on his face.

WATCH

ME

CYNTHIA
EDEN

Published by Cynthia Eden.

Cover art and design by: Pickyme/Patricia Schmitt

Proof-reading by: J. R. T. Editing

"Gwen trusts you," Will said. His blue eyes narrowed. "Use that trust. Get close to her. Stay close."

The guy had no idea what he was asking. "Your daughter has plenty of—"

"My daughter barely talks to me right now, but that doesn't mean I don't know what the hell is going on in her life. Remember that asshole she hooked up with a few months back? The one with the damn shady past that still gives me nightmares?"

Beneath the desk, Chance's hands clenched into fists. Yeah, he remembered the man. He also remembered how badly he'd wanted to rip the guy apart. Chance had seen what the fellow had done in the past—and he hadn't been about to let Ethan Barclay hurt Gwen.

No one hurts Gwen.

Well, that had been Chance's mantra. Then *he'd* been the one to break her heart.

"I'm worried about her. Gwen hasn't been the same since that jerk Barclay."

Chance cleared his throat. "Just because she had a bad break-up, that doesn't mean the woman needs a twenty-four hour bodyguard."

"What about the fact that someone is after her? Does *that* mean she needs protection?"

His body tensed. "You should have led with that shit, man." *And not come storming into my new office, telling me I had to take your job. Throwing your weight around and pulling your usual SOB routine.*

Will nodded. "I think it's Barclay. I think he's the one who's been tailing her. Some men can't let go, know what I mean?"

Unfortunately, he did. "Do you have evidence that it's him?"

Will's lips thinned. "No, but *someone* broke into my daughter's house. Someone has been calling her so much she's had to change her phone number twice in the last two months. Like I said, she's not talking much to me, but I am not about to let her be put at risk. I want you on the case. I want you close to my daughter."

But that might not be what Gwen wants.

"With Barclay's history…" Will sighed. "I won't take risks. I can't. Gwen has to be protected." He inclined his head toward Chance. "You want this business of yours to succeed, right? You and your friends want to become the most sought after bodyguard agency in D.C.? I can do that for you, and you know it. I can talk to the right people, I can give you more clients than you can even handle."

Yes, he knew the guy could. Just as he knew the wrong word from Will would have folks running *away* from his business.

Chance had been in security for years. Once upon a time, he'd even protected the president. He knew exactly how to stay close, how to shadow a client while looking for every possible threat. Hell, he'd been Will's chief of security for three years. Like that had been an easy job.

Protecting the president had been a cakewalk compared to life at Hawthorne Industries.

But Chance had finally branched out on his own. He and two of his closest friends had put all of their savings into this business. In D.C., the personal protection business was booming, and he was all set to tap into that boom.

The right words from Will...oh, yes, he'd be tapping in to that boom, all right.

And what about Gwen?

Her image flashed into his mind, an image that came to him far too often. Beautiful Gwen. "I didn't think you trusted me with your daughter." His words came out rougher than Chance had intended.

"I don't. I've seen the way you look at her." A muscle flexed in Will's jaw. "But I know...I know you'd keep her safe. She won't let anyone else stay close. Gwen's too smart. Like I said, she ditches every guard I put on her."

"And you think she won't ditch me?"

"I know you won't let her," Will said with certainty.

No, he wouldn't. Chance rubbed his jaw and felt the scrape of his five o-clock shadow. "I'll investigate," he finally said. "I'll see if anyone is after her or if you're just being a paranoid bastard." He didn't pull his punches with Will. Others did. Chance didn't.

Because he wasn't intimidated by the guy's money or power. Never had been. Never would be. "But let's be clear…I'm doing this for her. If she's in danger, then I will eliminate any threat. This isn't about you or any damn promises that you think you can make to me."

Looking satisfied, Will rose to his feet. "I am a paranoid bastard, but in my world, it pays to be that way." He lifted a brow. "You're taking the case?"

"I'm agreeing to watch Gwen." Chance had known he'd be taking the case the instant Will had uttered Gwen's name. He'd screwed up with her before, but this time…

Maybe I can get things right.

"Good, good." Will adjusted his already perfectly straight suit. "I want you to stay with her, twenty-four, seven. Keep the protection in place until you and your team find and *stop* the guy doing this to my daughter." He hesitated. "And just one more thing…don't tell Gwen about me, got it? I don't want her knowing I came to you."

Uh, that was quite the "one more thing" to ask. The guy wanted him to lie to Gwen?

"If she thinks you're working for me, she'll ditch you just like she has the others."

"I'm not exactly an amateur." And he'd watched Gwen before. She hadn't even known he'd been there.

"Don't tell her. Not unless it becomes absolutely necessary." The lines around Will's eyes deepened. "We both know she already hates me enough without adding this to the list."

Gwen and Will had a...contentious...relationship. Mostly because Will thought he should be able to control everyone and everything around him.

And Gwen didn't want to be controlled.

"Protect her. Find out who the hell is harassing my girl. And..." Will reached for his coat. "I'll make sure you have more clients than you can count."

"I can get my own clients." He didn't need the guy's help. But...Gwen...if she was in danger...

"Don't knock the help I can give you." Will held his stare. "Gwen's safety is priority one for me." He hesitated. "You're on the case?"

"I'll protect her." As if he'd ever be able to turn away from Gwen. *Not her.*

"Good." Will inclined his head toward him, then headed for the door. He slipped out of Chance's office and then Chance heard Will talking to someone else in the lobby.

Chance didn't move to follow the guy out. *Gwen.* Hell, was he really about to jump right back into the fire with her again? He'd barely walked away from her before. And as it was, every single night, the woman came to torment him in his dreams.

A light knock sounded at his door. He glanced up and waved in one of his partners, Lex Jenson. Lex came in and shut the door behind him. "So that's the big bad-ass."

Chance exhaled. "He just hired us to protect his daughter." He ran a hand over his face. "Or tried to." *But I'm not taking his money. Not for Gwen.*

Lex's eyes widened. "Gwen? Your Gwen?"

She wasn't his. That was the problem.

Or at least, she hadn't been…

"He thinks someone is after her." Chance reached for his coat. Why waste time? He knew where Gwen lived. He could start this case right now. "He wants us to find out who it is…and he wants Gwen to have twenty-four, seven protection until the guy is eliminated."

Chance brushed by Lex.

Lex grabbed his arm. "You told me how things went down the last time you two were together." His green eyes searched Chance's face. "I thought she never wanted to see you again. Isn't that the whole reason you agreed to jump ship and start this agency with me and Dev?"

No, that hadn't been the reason.

"Gwen is important." He stared grimly at his friend. "So let's not screw up."

Chance passed Lex. He grabbed for the door—

"As long as you don't screw her," Lex murmured. "I think we'll be golden."

His teeth snapped together. *Buddy, that's one promise I can't make.*

Because he'd already kept his hands off Gwen for far too long. She was the one woman he wanted the most. The one who tempted him and who could rip his control to shreds with just a look.

Twenty-four, seven protection…it was going to be hell.

Or heaven.

CHAPTER ONE

The music was loud, pounding. The crowd was thick. And Gwen Hawthorne danced right in the middle of that pack, waving her arms and trying to shout to her friends. She felt good right then. No worries. No fears. For just a few minutes, she was able to pretend that she was just like everyone else round her.

Even if she wasn't. Not really.

Because everyone else truly was happy. They weren't wearing a mask. Gwen…well, she knew she specialized in deception. It was a family trait.

Her dance partner—of the moment—pulled her close, smashing her body right against his. And, yes, the guy was good-looking, in a pretty-boy, too styled way. He was trying hard to grind against her hips and Gwen knew what the fellow was *hoping* would happen next.

A quick hook-up. Hot sex in the dark.

Not happening.

Gwen put her hands against his chest. "I need a break." She had to shout those words twice, then she pried herself out of his grasp.

"I can break with you, baby," he offered at once.

She shook her head. "Keep dancing."

His features tightened.

"I'm only here for the music," she told him, her voice firm. "Really, keep dancing." *And look for another hook-up partner.*

He nodded and, for a second, anger flashed in his gaze. But then a pretty redhead came by. She rolled her hips and the guy turned away from Gwen.

Sighing with more than a touch of relief, Gwen pushed her way through the crowd. It wasn't that she had anything against hot sex, but…well, she'd sworn off sex after her last disastrous experience. Or at least, she'd sworn off sex for the time being.

One hot hook-up had cost her too much. She wouldn't make the same mistake again.

She had almost reached the bar when she felt eyes on her. It started as kind of a vague awareness, an itch at the base of her neck and Gwen knew…someone was watching her.

Unfortunately, Gwen had experienced this same feeling all too often lately. It was seriously starting to creep her out.

She turned her head, sweeping her gaze over the men seated at the bar and then—

A pair of dark eyes — so dark they almost appeared black — caught her attention. Deep, dark eyes.

For a moment there, Gwen actually forgot to breathe.

He can't be here. He can't be here. He can't be —

Chance Valentine rose from his bar stool. He stalked toward her. Oh, crap, he most definitely was there. And he was coming right toward her.

As a general rule, courage had never been Gwen's strong suit. And since she'd pretty much made an absolute fool of herself the last time she'd crossed paths with Chance, she figured turning and running would be a good option for her.

So she turned.

She tried to run.

The crowd was too thick. The dancers too drunk. They were in her way and some guy caught her wrist, pulling her toward him because he must have thought her frantic moves were a cry for a dance partner.

They weren't. She just wanted to escape.

"You smell so good," her dance partner told her as he leaned in close. "You smell like — "

"Back the fuck off," a low, growling voice told the fellow as Chance stepped forward. Only Chance must have decided the guy wasn't backing off fast enough, because he grabbed the man's shoulder and shoved him away.

"Hey!" The younger, smaller man snarled. "What gives? You can't just—"

Chance, all six feet, three inches of him, glowered at the guy. "She's with me." Considering that Chance was seriously muscled and had to outweigh the other guy by at least fifty pounds, Gwen wasn't particularly surprised when the would-be-dancer backed away and disappeared into the crowd.

If only she could disappear so easily.

Instead, she decided to bluff things out. "Liar, liar," Gwen accused softly. Their bodies were far too close—courtesy of that crushing crowd. She was almost touching Chance and touching him would be a serious mistake.

The last time she'd touched him, Gwen had gotten burned.

His lips—a little cruel and far too sexy—curled a bit. "Running, were you?"

"I was simply going back to dance." She could lie, too. Besides, Chance—follow-the-rules, obey-orders-all-the-time Chance—he wasn't going to dance with her. Not in that pack. Not anyplace. "So if you don't mind…"

He caught her right hand in his. Looped his left behind her back and pulled her close. "I don't mind at all."

She stared up at him, totally lost. His dark hair was thick and a little long, brushing against his collar. A light line of stubble darkened his jaw. His face was just as handsome as she remembered — dammit — in a hard, almost brutal way. He had those dangerous looks that attracted women who should know better.

Women like her.

Deep, dark, let-me-fuck-you eyes. High cheekbones. A hard, square jaw. A faint scar sliced through his left eyebrow, but even that white line was sexy. Unfortunately, everything about Chance Valentine was sexy to Gwen.

And he was…dancing with her. Moving slowly. Sensuously. The music had changed. It wasn't some wild, blaring beat now. It was softer. Smoother. All about seduction. And his fingers were just above the curve of her ass.

"What are you doing?" Gwen asked. She hated that her voice sounded like a squeak.

Chance smiled. Her heart broke a little then. His smile did that to her — twisted her up and made her want things she knew she couldn't have.

"If you have to ask," Chance murmured, his voice a low rumble, "then my dancing is even shittier than I thought."

No, it wasn't. He was moving fluidly, holding her easily, and she wanted to get closer to him.

So she stepped away or, rather, she tried to step away. Chance didn't let her go far. *He rejected you once, Gwen. Don't give him the opportunity to do it again.* "What are you doing here?" Gwen rose onto her toes, trying to see over his shoulder. "This isn't your kind of place."

"Now how would you know that?"

"Because you don't exactly scream dance party scene." No, he screamed *danger* in big, red letters.

His head cocked to the side. "You really don't know me very well, Gwen."

Right…like that was her fault. She'd tried to learn his secrets. The guy wasn't the sharing sort.

"I saw you when I came in." His hold tightened on her. "The blond on the dance floor was nearly fucking you right there."

He'd been watching her that long?

"You left one guy…only to get caught by another. You sure seem popular here, Gwen."

She had to swallow to clear the lump in her throat. "It's a busy club. If you look around, you'll see that everyone is dancing here." Her chin notched up. "And I wasn't about to fuck the blond on the dance floor." She'd very clearly told him that she was only there to dance.

"Learned from last time, huh?"

At those low words, everything slowed down for her. Slowed down and got quiet. Because he had *not* just said that to her.

"It's not safe to screw a stranger you meet at a bar. But you learned that, didn't you?" His jaw was harder, his words rougher. He was angry.

So was she. "Let me go," Gwen said.

He gave a short, negative shake of his head.

"Let me go," Gwen said again, "Or I will start screaming. Want to see how fast the bouncers close in and drag you out of here?"

He was silent a moment. The heat from his touch seemed to sear her. Gwen held her breath and she got ready to scream.

He let her go.

Quickly, she stepped back. She bumped into the dancers behind her, and Gwen muttered an apology. Then she kept right on muttering apologies as she pushed her way through the crowd. She couldn't believe that Chance had just hurt her that way. To bring up Ethan. Yes, she knew hooking up with him had been a colossal mistake — one that still ripped at her heart.

But she didn't need Chance pointing out her past mistakes to her. No one was perfect, not even the mighty Chance.

She hurried back to her table, said her good-byes to her friends, and she grabbed her jacket. Gwen still had that too-aware feeling, as if someone was watching her.

Chance?

She didn't look around for him. Instead, she made a beeline for the exit. Gwen shoved open the door and headed out into the cold December night. December in D.C....that meant the politicians were mostly out of town and the snow was on the ground. Or, in this case, the snow was falling. Light snowflakes feathered down over her and Gwen shivered. She pulled her coat a bit closer and hunched her shoulders. She'd hail a cab and get the hell out of there. She lifted her hand—

Chance caught her fingers.

When she exhaled, the cold turned her breath into a little puff of smoke.

"I'm sorry," Chance said, that deep voice of his a rumble that she could almost feel. "I hurt you back there, and, believe me, that's the last thing I intended to do."

The snowflakes kept falling on them.

"I can be a jealous jerk sometimes," he told her as he stepped closer. "You should probably know that about me."

Cars were rushing by on the street. She could grab a taxi, no problem. But even though the cold was starting to make her toes tingle in her boots, Gwen didn't move. "Jealous?" It took an effort to get that one word out. Then she gave a strangled laugh, convinced he was mocking her. "You've never been jealous—"

"I wanted to punch the men who were dancing with you in that club. Shove them the hell away from you. *I* wanted to be the only one touching you."

She couldn't be hearing him correctly. The cold had frozen her ears and she wasn't hearing —

"And do you know how long I've wanted to beat the hell out of Ethan Barclay?"

Ethan. Her ex-lover. The man who'd taught her how very wrong it was to ever trust a sweet-talking stranger. The man she'd turned to out of desperation...

Because I couldn't have Chance.

Gwen shook her head.

"Ever since he had you." And he stepped even closer to her. So close she could feel the tempting warmth of his body again. "He had what he never should have touched."

She had no clue what was going on right then. Chance was saying things...the way he was looking at her...

"I wanted you." His head bent toward her. His lips were so close. "If anyone was going to fuck you, it should have been me."

This wasn't happening.

He sucked in a sharp breath. "But I screwed up. I know I did."

Yes, he had.

"I want another chance with you."

She was pretty sure her jaw dropped. Her whole body was shaking from the cold, though, so it was rather hard to tell for certain.

"You and me," Chance murmured. "Let's see what can happen between the two of us."

Gwen already had a pretty good idea of what would happen. An explosion. No, maybe an implosion. They'd touch. They'd go wild. It would be awesome.

But then the aftermath would come. She'd just be left with ashes.

Been there, done that.

She slipped away from him. Raised her hand. Got a taxi to miraculously stop in about ten seconds.

Chance just watched her with those dark eyes of his.

"Good-bye, Chance," she said as she reached for the cab's door. She'd learned her lesson before. Some fires burned too hot. It was better to be cold than to go up in flames.

She slid into the cab and mumbled her destination to the driver. When the cab eased away from the curb, Gwen told herself *not* to look back at Chance. But, dammit, she did.

The snow was falling on him. His hands were thrust deep into the pockets of his jacket. And he was just…staring after her.

Gwen shivered in the cab. She didn't know why Chance Valentine was suddenly back in her life, but she wasn't dumb enough to believe his reappearance was due to some overwhelming desire for her.

If only.

She knew how Chance felt about her. Chance and his control…the man never let anyone or anything break through that iron control of his. And he sure as hell wasn't coming after her because his need for her had grown too strong.

No, something else was happening. She just had to figure out what it was.

But if Chance is involved…it can't be good.

Chance had been her father's chief of security. The man who took care of any danger that arose. He had a well-deserved reputation for being a bad-ass.

So why was the bad-ass after her?

***

He watched the taxi drive away. Chance didn't even feel the icy touch of the snow around him. He seemed to be burning up from the inside. He'd screwed up in the club. A grade-A screw up. But he'd seen Gwen with those other men, and a white-hot jealousy had exploded within him.

His phone was ringing. He yanked it out of his pocket even as he stalked down the street. "Valentine," he snapped.

"I thought the whole point…" Lex's mocking voice said, "was to keep a twenty-four, seven watch on her. Not to have your pretty blonde lady run away as fast as she could."

Lex could be such a dick. "You're tailing her, right?"

"I'm behind the cab right now."

Chance grunted as he climbed into his car. "I'll be at her apartment before she is."

"Cause that's not going to make her uncomfortable," Lex murmured.

"I understand Gwen. She ran tonight because I was an idiot." He slammed his door. "I said the wrong thing, but I've got this."

"You'd better, man. With the power her father has, the guy could make or break our business." Lex wasn't mocking anymore. "We need his clout, you know it. So if I need to take over this case, if there's too much between you and Gwen for this to work out—"

"Gwen is mine." He hadn't meant to say those words. Had he? "I've got this," Chance repeated. "Trust me." *And we don't need Will Hawthorne. We can make this business a success on our own.*

Lex's sigh traveled over the line. "All right, but just remember, I'm here as backup, if you need me."

He disconnected the call. He didn't need Lex's help. Not then. What he needed was to stop seeing the image of Gwen's pain-filled green eyes in his mind. When she'd looked up at him, the hurt plain to see in her gorgeous gaze—well, she'd nearly gutted him. And the woman had no idea. She thought he was screwing around with her? Hell, no. Every word he'd said that night had been the truth.

As much as he could, he only wanted to give Gwen the truth.

He cut through the city, taking the path that Chance knew would get him to her apartment long before the cabbie arrived. His fingers were tight around the wheel. He'd gone into that club, he'd tracked her there when her apartment had been empty, and he'd been so pissed when he saw her slammed against that prick on the dance floor. Her movements had been pure sex, and the dumb-ass with her had been holding her tightly.

He'd looked at them and thought...

The fuck, no. When Gwen leaves, she's only leaving with me.

He wasn't going to wreck things with her again.

He cut through the falling snow and was soon at Gwen's place. He parked his car, turned up the collar on his coat, and headed toward her building. He propped his back against the bricks there, standing in the shadows, as he surveyed the scene. No one else was out. No neighbors. This area was far too isolated for his peace of mind. Especially if Ethan Barclay really was trying to hunt Gwen.

He kept his hands shoved into his pockets. He'd have to play this one very carefully with Gwen...if he messed up again, there was no way she would let him get close.

The cab turned onto the street. He could see its lights clearly. The wheels slowed in front of Gwen's building. The back door opened and Gwen slid out. Before she'd even reached the sidewalk, the cabbie had already left.

Gwen headed straight for her apartment building. She didn't even look his way. There were too many places to hide on that street. Too much darkness. He stepped forward, ready to call out to her but—

She reached for the door to her building. Even as she pulled it open, someone else was shoving it back toward her. Someone was shoving *Gwen* back and knocking her to the ground.

Chance flew toward them, yelling Gwen's name. He could make out a figure in black— black pants, black shirt, black ski mask. A big guy who was crouched over Gwen. She was fighting the fellow, punching at him.

The hell, no.

The attacker glanced up just as Chance threw a punch right at the bastard. The man flew back, slamming into the ground. Chance immediately reached for Gwen. He pulled Gwen to her feet. "Baby, are you okay?"

He heard the thud of retreating footsteps. Chance looked to the right and saw the guy racing away into the night.

"He's got my bag!" Gwen said. "He took it—"

Swearing, Chance gave chase. He rushed after the bastard, his legs pistoning fast. He could see the jerk up ahead, nearing a parked van and—

The van's lights flashed on right then and the engine growled to life. *Sonofabitch—a getaway car!* The side of the van flew open and the guy in black leapt inside.

In the next instant, the van came careening straight for Chance.

"*Run, Chance!*" Gwen's scream—and that scream was coming from just a few feet away. He looked over his shoulder and saw her standing in the middle of the street. The van's lights were on him, on her, and, dammit, that van was rushing far too fast toward them.

He ran—to her. Chance grabbed Gwen and they leapt out of the road and flew toward the sidewalk. They hit the ground and he made sure to take the force of the impact, and then they were rolling, spinning away from the street as the van roared past them.

He could smell burning rubber and exhaust. He could hear the van's growling engine. And when he looked up, Chance saw the back of the van and its glowing red tail-lights. The vehicle screeched down the road and made a hard right turn at the intersection.

Chance sure as shit hoped Lex had just seen what went down. Lex had better tail that van and catch that jerk.

"Are you hurt?" Gwen whispered.

He looked back down at her. They were under a street light and the glow fell on them. Her eyes looked even bigger than before. Her lips were parted. Such red, full lips. Lips that he thought about far too much.

But then, he thought of Gwen too much. Beautiful, perfect Gwen. Gwen with her wide eyes, her delicate nose, and those cheeks that looked as if they were made of glass. Gwen's body was all sensual curves—curves that drove him out of his head and made him itch to touch her.

Except…she wasn't for him. That was what he'd thought, anyway. Too good. A woman like her would shatter if he touched her.

Only she wasn't shattering just then.

"Are you hurt?" Gwen asked again.

Hell, that was supposed to be his line. He shook his head.

"Good," she whispered. "I'm so glad. I-I was worried—"

He kissed her. Maybe it was because of the adrenaline. Maybe it was because of the desire that he was so sick of holding in check around her. Maybe the why didn't matter.

Chance let go of his control. His mouth crashed onto hers. Onto those full, make-me-beg lips. His tongue thrust into her mouth and he tasted her the way he'd been *dying* to for so long.

The lust he felt for her filled him. His cock stretched, aching to sink into her. And he kept kissing her, right there on the ground, with the snow falling around them. He kissed her hard. He kissed her deep. He kissed her the way he wanted to fuck her.

And he knew that they'd just crossed a line, a point of no return.

Gwen Hawthorne was going to be his, and anyone who tried to take her from him, anyone who tried to hurt her...he would fucking destroy.

CHAPTER TWO

"It was a mugging, Chance. Just a mugging. Unfortunately, those happen in D.C., just like they happen in plenty of other big cities." Gwen was proud of the fact that her voice sounded all nice and normal. Especially considering how very far from normal she actually felt.

They were in her apartment. The cops had already come and left—the uniformed officer hadn't seemed overly optimistic that her attacker would be caught.

And while the fresh-faced cop had jotted down notes, Chance had glared at the guy. *If looks could kill…*

"You don't know that it was just a mugging," Chance argued. "We can't be sure of that." He was currently stalking in front of her couch.

He was sexy when he stalked. All tall, dark, and menacing.

He's even sexier when he kisses me.

She still couldn't believe *that* had happened. He'd kissed her on the street, with the snow all around them. And he'd wanted her. No way had she missed that too-telling sign. It would have been nearly impossible to miss the huge swell of his arousal pressing into her.

"The cops should patrol your neighborhood. Keep guards on you."

That was the last thing she wanted. She'd already spent too many years being under guard, or rather, under the too watchful eyes of her father's security team.

Speaking of her father… "You're not going to tell him, are you? You aren't planning to tell my father about the mugging?"

He stopped pacing. "You were attacked. The guy was waiting at your place —"

"You heard the cop! He thought the guy was probably just casing the neighborhood. I was the unlucky one who happened to be here, at the wrong time."

A muscle flexed in his jaw. "What would have happened if I hadn't been here?"

"H-he would have taken my purse and left."

He shook his head. "You really believe that?"

No. Yes. She didn't know. Gwen rose to her feet. Closed the distance between them. "Why were you here?" He'd burst out of the darkness like an avenging angel.

His eyelids flickered. "I couldn't let things end like that between us. I needed to…to talk with you."

"So you followed me home?"

"No, I beat you home. And that's how I know that jerk was waiting inside the building — he was waiting for you."

Goosebumps rose on her arms.

Chance's gaze slid toward her door. The door she'd triple locked. "He got away with your keys. I'll get my men to change the locks here first thing. And the locks at your gallery. You told the cop that there weren't any credit cards in your bag, but are you sure about that?"

"I only had a little cash in my bag. Nothing more." Her shoulders straightened. "And I don't need your guys coming to fix my locks. I know how to hire a locksmith. I can easily take care of that on my own."

Silence. His gaze swung back to her. Oh, my, but that stare of his glittered with intensity. "Has anything else like this happened to you recently?"

Gwen forced herself to keep holding his stare. "Has someone mugged me, you mean? No, this is a first — "

His hand lifted and curled around her arm. At that touch, her heartbeat instantly went into a double-time beat.

"Has anyone given you trouble? Have you noticed anyone following you?"

She jerked a bit at his questions.

"Gwen?"

Her eyes narrowed on him. "You have your own PI business now."

He stared back at her. "It's a bodyguard business. We specialize in high-end protection. The discrete, save-your-ass variety. But we do occasionally handle…other types of security cases."

He'd saved her ass tonight. She sucked in a deep breath, one that seemed to chill her lungs. "Has my father been to see you?"

"What does he have to do with anything?"

"He wants me protected." No, that wasn't quite true. "He wants me in a cage. So the world can't hurt me. And so I can't see the world." He was still touching her, and she was far too conscious of his touch. "It's because of Ethan, isn't it? My dad is still worried about him."

"Ethan's a sick bastard."

Her stomach knotted. "Ethan can't get close to me. I have a restraining order against him, remember? Besides, he's not after me. I know that's what my father thinks, but he's wrong. I haven't seen or heard from the guy in six months. Not since…"

Silence. The kind of silence that she hated.

But maybe she needed to say these words. "Not since you burst into my bedroom and beat the hell out of him." Talk about a memory that had been permanently seared into her brain.

***

He tossed the ski mask onto his bed. That bastard had come out of nowhere. Had the asshole been hiding in the dark? Waiting for Gwen?

Only he'd gotten to play the hero. Rushing to the rescue.

And Gwen...Gwen had no clue that the guy was as twisted as they came.

He marched toward his desk. Keyed up the computer. Gwen's purse was on the floor beside his chair, and he kicked it out of the way. He hadn't cared about the purse, but it gave him a good cover. If she'd called the cops, they would just think he'd been mugging her. They wouldn't know what he'd really been doing.

No one would know. After all, he was very good at this type of work. An expert.

He typed in his password. Got the system linked and up and running and...

The feed slipped right up on his screen. He smiled when he saw the interior of Gwen's apartment. But that smile froze on his lips when he realized that Gwen Hawthorne wasn't alone.

Fucking bastard.

This was really going to mess up the plans that had been put in place.

***

Gwen shook her head. Her thick, blonde hair slid over her shoulders. "That's not exactly a scene that a girl can forget." She swallowed. "I had to pull you off him."

His hands had clenched into fists. Hell. Chance forced his body to relax. Ethan wasn't there. Gwen was safe.

That one night was etched in his memory. The night his self-control had broken. He'd already told Gwen all about Ethan's past by that point. Her father had been the one to give Chance that particular dirty job. He'd had to break the news to her. Chance had stood there while pain and horror flashed across Gwen's face.

After that, she'd broken up with Ethan Barclay. Kicked the guy's ass out of her life.

Chance had gone to Gwen's apartment that fateful night. Gwen had been hurting — *because of me* — and he'd just wanted to take her pain away. But he hadn't. Gwen hadn't wanted him there. She'd told him to leave, that she had to be alone. Chance had roamed the city and then found himself back at her apartment, staring up at the window. He'd hated for her to be in pain. Hated the thought of her tears.

Then he'd seen Ethan's car parked near the corner of her street. His instincts had gone into overdrive and he'd found himself racing to her building.

"Why did you come back that night?" Gwen asked him now.

He rolled his shoulders, trying to push away tension that just wouldn't vanish. "I knew you were hurting, and I didn't want you to be alone. I was coming back to…talk. And then I saw his car." His breath eased out. "I was at your front door when I heard you scream." He'd broken that damn door and rushed inside. Gone straight to the bedroom. He'd kicked in that door, too, and when he'd see Gwen in bed and that bastard Ethan looming over her…

"I'd never seen you like that." Now her voice was soft. Her eyes slid over his face. "You just…erupted. I had to pull you off him."

Because he'd wanted to destroy the bastard. "He broke into your home."

She nodded. "I sure didn't invite the guy back. After what you'd told me, did you believe for a second that I had?"

With her scream ringing in his ears, he hadn't exactly been thinking straight. Just feeling. Following a primitive instinct to protect.

"Ethan said he came here that night to talk with me. Because I'd been ignoring his phone calls. He wanted to tell me the truth about his past."

Fuck that. "The truth is that he's a criminal. A bastard who beat his ex-girlfriend up so badly that she wound up in the hospital. I wasn't going to let him do that to you." A simple fact. "I wasn't—"

"You were doing your job. Protecting the boss's daughter. That was your thing, right? Your assignment. To eliminate all possible threats."

It had been one hell of a lot more than an assignment.

"I can't help but wonder…are you doing your job now, too?"

If he said that her father had come to his office, Chance had no doubt that she would kick him out of her home right then. He didn't want that to happen and he also didn't want to lie to her. So, very carefully, he said, "I will do anything necessary to protect you. Always. From any threat." He held her gaze. "Now I think you're the one who needs to start sharing your secrets. That man tonight…was that the first time you've had an encounter like that? Is something else going on? Is—"

She paced toward her window. Stared out. "I've gotten…phone calls, okay? Late night phone calls from numbers that I don't recognize. Numbers that I can't trace. The callers would never say anything. Just silence. I turned the phones off but…" One shoulder lifted and fell. "When I'd turn them back on, there would be dozens of messages. Messages made of nothing but silence and the occasional whisper that I couldn't even understand." She looked back at him. "It was probably just some kids playing games, but it made me nervous, so I got a new number."

He waited.

"I got a new number a few times," she confessed. "But…but I haven't seen anyone. No one has been in my house or at my gallery." The gallery…*her* gallery. The place she'd built from the ground up. She didn't just showcase her work there. She showed the work of up and coming artists. She gave them a chance to shine in D.C. She loved that damn gallery. *But lately…I've been nervous there. I hate to work alone at the gallery late at night. My spine tingles and I wonder…am I really alone?* Gwen cleared her throat. "I just…I've had some kids prank calling me." She rubbed her arms. "I can't go running for help every time my phone rings."

He crossed to her side. Stood close, but didn't touch her. His control was already a near thing and one touch might push him over the line. "You can run to me any time you want."

He heard her breath catch. "Months pass," she whispered, "and I don't see you. Now, suddenly, you're back in my life?"

"You're the one who told me to leave." Shit. He hadn't meant to say those words. But they were right there. Right between them. When he'd burst into her apartment, when he'd put Ethan in the hospital, she'd stared at him as if Chance had been a stranger.

Stay away from me. Her desperate whisper had haunted him for too many nights.

Until he couldn't stay away any longer.

"I was kind of in the middle of a break down right then. My ex had just broken into my apartment and you'd gone all crazy bad-ass fighter on me. Things like that will shake up a woman." She licked her lips. "I...missed you."

Because he'd been her confidant. For years. Her father hadn't let many people get close to Gwen, and when Chance came on board, Gwen had gravitated toward him. She'd been living at her father's place back then, and they'd shared late-night dinners. They'd gone for early morning runs. He'd gotten used to her being the first person he saw when he woke up in the morning, and the last sight he had before bed.

And she got beneath my skin.

Then things had changed. One night...on Christmas Eve, he'd been weak. He'd almost given in to his need for Gwen. Too late, he'd pulled back, but he'd hurt her.

Gwen had moved out of her father's house. A few months later, she'd fucked that bastard Ethan. And she'd seen Chance for the man he really was.

Stay away from me.

Now she reached out. Her fingers skimmed along his jaw.

Did she have any clue how long he'd wanted her touch? How he'd dreamed about her? Dreamed of the things he wanted to do to her? "I got tired of staying away," he told her, his voice close to a growl.

She inched closer to him. "You're not working for my father anymore. So that whole...not crossing the work line doesn't apply any longer, right?"

"We can cross any line we want." He wanted to cross every line with her right then. He wanted to take her, right there, to claim her as he should have done so long ago. Then there would have been no fear from Gwen. No threat from Ethan. It would have just been the two of them.

"I want you," Gwen said, staring up at him. "But I'm afraid."

No, no, *no*. He didn't want her afraid of him. "I'd never hurt you."

Her smile was bittersweet. "You could destroy me, and you'd never have to lift a hand to do it."

"Gwen—"

"Ethan didn't matter, not enough to break me. You...you're different." She backed away, almost hitting the window. "You should go now."

The last thing he wanted to do was leave. He wanted to stay right there with her. All night long.

"I'm safe. You protected me." Her head inclined toward him as her hair brushed lightly over her shoulders. "Again. So you can go home knowing that I'm all good for the night."

"Or I could stay here, with you, and make absolutely certain that you're…good…for the night."

Her pupils expanded. For an instant, he saw desire blazing in her eyes. His heart thundered in his chest because he was so very close to the one thing he wanted most.

"I'm not going to make a mistake again." She shook her head. "So for tonight, it's good-bye."

"But your locks — you need them changed —"

"I'll secure the deadbolt again when you leave. And I'll put a chair under the door."

She's kicking me out. His back teeth clenched, but he leaned forward, and, after a tense moment, he pressed a quick kiss to her forehead. "If anything happens, if you get scared, call me."

"I will."

She walked him to the door. Gazed at him a little wistfully as he slipped out of her apartment, then she shut the door in his face.

Hell. Getting back into Gwen's good graces wasn't going to be nearly as easy as he'd hoped.

***

Gwen was being a good girl. She'd just sent that bastard on his way. Locked the door. Now she was pacing her apartment. Looking a little lost.

And completely alone.

He leaned toward his screen. She had no idea the hell that was coming her way. She thought she was safe.

There was no safety.

Before he was done, Gwen would know that. Gwen would know what it was like to lose everything.

Every fucking thing. It was his job to make sure she suffered before the end came.

***

Gwen's light was still on.

Chance sat in his car, darkness all around him, and peered up at her apartment. He could see her silhouette near the window.

A light rap came from the passenger side of the car. He'd known that Lex was there, so he unlocked the door and let the guy inside.

"Huh…kind of figured you'd be doing the surveillance from *inside* her apartment," Lex said as he handed Chance a burger from the local fast food joint. "Guess you struck out tonight, huh?"

"Screw off," Chance told him as he tossed the wrapped burger onto the dashboard. "I want to know how the hell you lost that van."

Lex winced. "The clubs are all letting out, man. Traffic two roads over is a bitch. The guy knew that. He planned it. He disappeared in that maze and there was no catching him. At least…not yet."

Chance waited.

"I've got some connections we can use. I'm already pulling strings to get access to the traffic cams in the area. We might get lucky and spot the guy on video. If we do, we'll find him. The guy only slipped away for the time being. He's not gone for good."

He'd better not be.

"So are we still looking at the ex? Ethan Barclay? You think the guy got obsessed and can't let go?"

"Ethan has a history of obsession." And violence. "Three years ago, his ex-fiancée was killed in a car crash, one week after she'd broken up with him. Then he had another girlfriend, Marjorie…she wound up in the hospital, with broken ribs and a concussion. She filed charges against him, but then…hell, I don't know what happened. She dropped the charges and vanished. He got away clean." His fingers tapped against the steering wheel. "So, yeah, I think it's safe to say the man may have one serious problem with rejection."

Lex whistled. "Sounds like a serious asshole."

"Ethan has had plenty of brushes with the law, but nothing has stuck. The guy has been in and out of jail more times than I can count. Or at least, he was, until he turned eighteen. Since then—"

"He's gotten smarter about avoiding arrest," Lex guessed.

Chance nodded. "That's what I figure." The guy sure hadn't gone legit.

Gwen's lights turned off.

Chance tensed.

"Um, man, are you sure he's the only one obsessed?"

Very slowly, Chance turned his head to stare at his friend.

"What I mean..." Lex rushed to say. "What I mean is that until we have proof that Ethan is our guy, we have to keep our options open."

Damn straight they did.

Lex bit into his burger. "And I also meant..." He mumbled around the food, "that you've got it bad for her."

Tell me something I don't know.

He stared back up at Gwen's window.

***

Her phone rang. Gwen turned in her bed, moving so that her gaze fell on the phone that rested nearby. The phone was on the nightstand and when it rang again, it vibrated, moving slightly against the wooden surface.

She reached out and her fingers curled around the phone. She swiped her finger across the screen. Gwen didn't recognize the number. She shouldn't answer it—

She did.

"Hello?" Gwen put the phone to her ear.

Nothing.

Another one of those damn calls.

"This isn't funny," she snapped. "Stop calling me. I'm sick of this game, got it?"

She heard the quick exhalation of breath and then… "Never said it was a game."

The voice was a low, rough rasp. Her heart actually stopped when the man spoke.

"Who is this?" Gwen demanded.

"You smelled good tonight." He was still talking in that low, raspy voice, as if he wanted to disguise himself. "Like vanilla. You use that vanilla lotion, don't you? Put it all over your body."

She pulled the covers closer. She did use vanilla lotion. She kept it on the vanity in her bathroom.

"Scared?" He laughed then. "Are you going to sink under the covers and wish this monster would go away?"

Sink under the covers…

She had sunk beneath the covers.

"Too bad, princess. I'm not some bad dream you can wish away." His voice roughened. "You're not going to escape from me."

"Who is th-this?" She hated that her voice trembled.

"I like those panties you're wearing. They're sexy. But you should have ditched the shirt."

Before she'd climbed into bed, she'd pulled on a pair of bright red panties and an old college t-shirt.

He saw me. It was suddenly hard to breathe. *Sink under the covers…*

She was inching even deeper beneath those covers. Dear God…was he watching her right then? Was he in her apartment? "Leave me alone," she told him.

"Never," he promised.

The line went dead.

The silence was suddenly too thick. Too terribly thick and consuming. Every muscle in her body was tight because she was afraid that she wasn't alone.

She'd woken once before and found a man in her bedroom. Ethan had reached out to her and she'd screamed.

Was he back? Had he come for her again?

Maybe her father had been right. Dammit, she hated it when he was right and—

Something scratched against her window. With a sharp cry, Gwen leapt from the bed and raced out of her bedroom.

CHAPTER THREE

Chance's phone rang. He frowned down at the screen, but he answered quickly. "Valentine—"

"He's watching me."

Chance would have recognized Gwen's voice anywhere. Anytime. But he sure didn't like the fear that trembled in her words.

"I-I searched my apartment, twice, but the things he said when he called me…he has to be here. He has to be close. He's watching me."

"Gwen, baby, slow down." But he was already reaching for his car door. He motioned to Lex, covered the phone and said… *"Keep an eye out."*

Then he was leaping out of the car. The snow was falling even harder. "Tell me what's happening."

"He called again." She wasn't slowing down. Her words were shooting out in rapid-fire succession. "What he said…he had to see me. He knew how I smelled."

Chance was in her apartment building and running for the stairs.

"He knew what I was wearing. My…my panties. The t-shirt."

Chance was on the second level of stairs.

"He could see me," she said, her words rough. "But I can't find him. I can't!"

Chance was on her floor. "Baby, open your door. I'm here."

He could hear the quick thud of her footsteps. Then the door flew open and Gwen was there. She saw him and she threw herself against him. His arms closed around her, the movement as natural as breathing. She trembled against him.

Gwen still had her phone gripped tightly in her hand as she eased back to stare up at him. "He was watching, but he isn't here. He isn't."

He could hear her fear and he hated that she was so terrified. *No one should do this to her.*

Without her heels, Gwen stood at only five foot four in front of him. She seemed far too delicate standing there. Too breakable.

"He said I wasn't going to escape from him." She glanced back over her shoulder and into her apartment. Chance realized that she'd turned on every light in the place. "He said I'd never get away."

The SOB was dead wrong.

***

An hour later, Chance had Gwen safely installed at his place. He'd sent Lex to thoroughly search her apartment *and* to go ahead and change her locks. Chance had done a sweep before they'd left the place, and he knew that the guy harassing Gwen hadn't actually been *inside* her home. At least, not when the jerkoff had called her.

But he was watching her.

Which meant the guy had probably wired the place. Chance didn't think the incident from earlier had been a mugging gone wrong. Hell, no. He thought that bastard had just planted cameras or bugs at Gwen's place. Only she'd arrived home before the guy could make his getaway. And with Gwen so close, the guy hadn't been able to resist grabbing her.

You are going to pay, asshole.

"I could have stayed in a hotel. Or even gone to my father's place." Gwen's arms were wrapped around her stomach. "You didn't have to bring me here."

"Yes, I did." Because he wanted her in his house. He wanted her close.

Gwen was wearing a pair of faded jeans that hugged her hips and ass beautifully. Her old college t-shirt was weathered and looked far too sexy on her. Her hair was loose, and it fell over her shoulders. He thought she'd never looked more beautiful.

Shit, pull it back, man!

The woman had been threatened, harassed, and the last thing she needed was his lust right then, too.

So pull the hell back. Give her the protection she needs.

He pointed to the hallway. "My room's on the right. Go on in and get some sleep. I know you have to be dead on your feet."

Gwen didn't move. "Where will you sleep?"

His lips quirked. "The couch."

"No, Chance, you—"

"Baby, I've slept on plenty worse." Especially back in his soldier days. When he'd been a fresh recruit for Uncle Sam, he'd slept anywhere and everywhere, and often woken to the sound of gunfire. "Sleep in my bed, and I'll bunk down out here. I swear, you won't have a thing to worry about from me."

She hesitated, but then gave a quick nod.

When Gwen started to pass him, Chance's hand lifted and his fingers curled around her arm. "I'll need your phone. If that creep calls back, I'll handle him." And he'd also get his buddy Dev to try and trace down those calls. He and Lex had plenty of military and security training. And Devlin Shade was their tech expert.

Dev could hack his way into pretty much any piece of information.

She gave him the phone, but she didn't move away. "I've been wondering..." Her head tilted to the side as she studied him. "How did you get to my place so fast?"

Ah, he'd figured that question would come up, sooner or later. He'd rather hoped for later. "This is the part where I get to confess that I hadn't left."

"You were...watching me?"

"I had a bad feeling." True enough. "I just wanted to stay around a little bit, in case you needed me."

Her lashes fell, covering her eyes. "You seem to make a habit of saving me."

"I just don't want to see you hurt."

She swallowed. "My father...hell, he'll have a field day with this. He was convinced Ethan was after me. I have a restraining order on the guy and I haven't seen Ethan in months, so I thought he had to be wrong. Or maybe I just wanted him to be wrong." Her fingers brushed through her hair in a weary gesture. "Now my dad's going to insist I get a body guard and—" Her fingers stilled. A faint smile curved her lips. "I guess I have you."

Always. But he didn't say the word.

"Can I hire you, Chance? Will you keep up that habit of saving me...just until we figure out what's happening?" She shivered and said, "The man on the phone…he was talking about my panties. About them being sexy and he said he'd never let me go." Her lashes lifted. He could easily read the emotion in her gaze. "I'm scared."

And I want to destroy that bastard.

"Tell me your price."

Her words were eerily like her father's. Only…there was no price to pay. "Go to sleep," Chance told her. "You don't have to worry about anything tonight. I already told you, I'm not going to let you be hurt."

She started to speak, but then seemed to change her mind. Gwen gave a little nod and headed for the bedroom. He watched her walk away, his knees locked so he wouldn't give in to the urge to trail after her.

"If you need me…" His voice came out gravel rough. "Just call out."

Her hand lifted and her fingers curled around the door frame. Gwen glanced back over her shoulder. "Are you my guardian angel?"

Hell, no. His thoughts were far too sinful, and he was more like the devil who couldn't let her go. "Good night, Gwen."

"Good night," she whispered and then she disappeared into his bedroom.

***

He'd followed Gwen back to Chance's place. The prick Chance Valentine lived in a far more isolated location in the city. An old warehouse that Chance had converted into a home.

He'd already scoped the place out before, so he knew security was everywhere at that place. Chance and his little gadgets. The guy must think he was so damn smart.

Not smart enough.

Because if I can't get inside to dear Gwen, I'll just make Gwen come to me.

Playtime was over. He'd warned Gwen. The real party was about to begin.

"And it's going to be hot," he whispered.

***

She'd never been in Chance's home before. And everywhere she looked, Gwen saw Chance. His touch. His presence. She could practically feel him, all around her.

Almost as if he were in bed with her.

He wasn't, of course. He was down the hallway. Playing protector because she'd totally freaked out back at her apartment. But when a stalker called and basically threatened you, wasn't a little freak out normal? Gwen sure thought so.

And she also thought that sleep was about a million miles away.

She shoved off the covers. She was still wearing her jeans and her t-shirt. After that phone call, she'd been a little gun shy about just stripping off her clothes. Biting her lip, Gwen tiptoed toward the door. She'd been in the bedroom for over an hour, staring up at the ceiling, trying to decide why someone would want to make her life hell.

So surely Chance had fallen asleep in that time, right?

She opened the door and crept down the hallway. Her bare toes curled against the wooden floor. He'd turned off all the lights so she kept her hand against the wall as she walked. Gwen didn't hear him so she figured that had to mean Chance was sleeping—

"Where are you going?"

Or not.

She jumped, then automatically put her hand over her heart, as if that movement could somehow calm its frantic beat. "Jeez, Chance, were you trying to scare me to death?"

He turned on the lamp near the sofa. She noticed that he was sitting up and staring straight at her. He'd taken off his shirt and her gaze couldn't help but dip down and take in all of those wonderful muscles. It was almost a crime for a man to look that good.

"Gwen…"

She snapped her gaze back up to his face. "I couldn't get to sleep, so I was just going to grab something to drink. I didn't mean to wake you up."

"You didn't wake me."

Gwen took a few quick steps toward him.

"I was wide awake," he continued. "Sitting in here and thinking about how close you were to me."

She stopped taking those steps.

"I was trying to play the gentleman and leave you alone, but then you opened the door and you came to me."

She thought about retreating.

"Do you have any idea..." Chance asked her, voice roughening. "How much I want you?"

In that moment, she wished for the darkness. She wanted him to turn off the light because it would be so much easier to bare her soul in the darkness. But the light was on and maybe it was time to stop being afraid. "I offered myself to you before." Because she'd wanted him for so long. "You told me you weren't interested."

His hand clenched around the arm of the couch. "The hell I did. I told you I worked for your father and that I was supposed to keep my hands *off* you."

"Because you were worried that you'd get fired if you were caught screwing the boss's daughter."

Chance rose, standing to his full, impressive height. As he walked toward her, his body blocked the light from that lamp. He was a tall shadow, coming right at her. "I knew I'd be the one screwed," Chance said, voice deepening even more, "if I had you. Because once wouldn't be enough for me. If I had you, I wouldn't ever be able to let you go."

Gwen shook her head. She'd misheard. It was late. She was awake, but tired and —

"You weren't ready for what I'd need from you. You still aren't."

Now she bristled. "What about what I need?"

He stopped in front of her. "What do you need?"

Oh, hell. "Back then, I needed you. You were the man I wanted, the man I —" Gwen stopped herself, just in time. Stopped herself before she made a seriously damning confession about how he was the man she'd loved.

But Chance pushed, asking, "The man you…what?"

Careful now, Gwen said, "You were the man I wanted in my bed. You rejected me. You sent me away —"

"I didn't exactly know you'd go jumping into Ethan's bed!"

He'd gone too far. Heat stung her cheeks, then ice seemed to coat her skin. Gwen turned on her heel and started marching for the door. Not

the bedroom, but his front door because she
wanted to get the hell away from him.

"I'm sorry." Chance wrapped his arms
around her and pulled Gwen back up against
him. "Shit, baby, I'm sorry. I can be a total
asshole."

"Total," she agreed.

"You don't know what it did to me. To find
out you were with him...to go into that bedroom
and see—"

Her eyes squeezed shut. "I slept with him
months after your big rejection. *Months*. And
here's a big newsflash for you. He wasn't the first
man I ever slept with, and he won't be the last,
either."

She could feel him stiffen behind her.

"We aren't together, Chance. So what I do
and who I do it with...that's none of your
business."

"You think I don't know that?" His breath
blew over her ear and a shiver skated down
Gwen's body. "But the problem is...I feel too
much when you're close. I get so fucking jealous
of any man near you. And I'm tired of playing by
the rules. Tired of keeping my hands off..."

His hands weren't off, though. They were on
her, and they seemed to burn right through her
clothes.

"When I want to touch you more than I want
anything else."

Then he… he kissed her neck. She hadn't realized just how sensitive that spot was, not until that moment. But when she felt the press of his lips against her nape, her knees did a little jiggle. Her nipples tightened. And her sex ached.

I've wanted him for so long.

Adrenaline poured through her blood. And maybe it was that adrenaline rush that was making her reckless, but Gwen found herself turning in his arms. She stared up at his face. The face that had haunted her nights.

He wanted her.

She'd longed for him.

"I'm sorry," he told her. "I'm an asshole. I just…I want you so much. And the thought of you with another drives me insane."

She didn't want to imagine him with another woman, so Gwen could understand that part. For too long, she'd only imagined Chance…*with me.*

And in that moment, he was with her. They were alone. The air thick with tension. Need.

So…why not take what they both needed? Why not give in, just once?

"Kiss me." The words whispered from her.

And he did. His mouth took hers. Seduced hers. She'd already known that Chance could kiss, but this time, things were different. She could taste the desire in his kiss. His tongue stroked into her mouth. Tempted. Took. She rose onto her toes and kissed him back just as desperately. Seduction gave way to growing passion. To a need that they'd both denied for far too long.

He backed her up and her shoulders hit the wood of the door. Gwen didn't care. Her nails were digging into his shoulders and she was fighting to get closer to him.

Because just like...*that*...the desire she felt for him wasn't controlled any longer. There was no control. There was only passion.

Her hips arched against him. The long, hard length of his cock pressed against her. She wanted him in her. Wanted them both to be racing toward the edge of oblivion as the pleasure took over.

He grabbed the hem of her shirt. Pushed it up. Threw it someplace. Then his fingers were sliding under the edge of her bra. She needed that bra gone so that she could feel him and —

The bra was gone. He bent his head and his mouth closed over her breast. Her eyes squeezed closed and a moan tore from her when he started to suck her nipple. She was pretty sure that her panties were getting drenched.

And they'd just gotten started.

But she'd always known it would be this way. The intensity, the attraction, had been there from the very beginning. Sometimes, she'd just looked at Chance and wanted.

His tongue stroked her. He scored her with his teeth. Her hips jerked frantically against him because she needed to be closer to him.

He kissed his way to her other breast. "You taste delicious."

He was driving her wild! Gwen's eyes flew open.

But even as he kissed her nipple, his fingers had slid down to the snap of her jeans. He yanked open that snap. Slid down her zipper, and then his hand pushed into the opening there. Down, down his fingers went and so did her jeans. They fell to the floor, and, frantic, she kicked them away. Then she widened her stance because she wanted him to—

He stroked her through her panties.

He had to tell that she was wet for him. She was so eager and her breath just panted out. His index finger traced over the red silk between her legs. That teasing touch wasn't close to enough. She needed more. She needed deeper. "Chance!"

His head lifted. He stared down at her, and the dark lust on his face should have given her pause. He was staring down at her as if he could eat her alive.

Was she staring at him the same way?

Still gazing at her, his fingers slid under the edge of her panties. Those long, strong fingers— slightly callused, a little rough—pushed between her folds. His index finger slid into her and she started to close her eyes again—

"Keep looking at me."

She bit her lip because she was about to go crazy, but she managed to keep looking into his eyes. That finger of his slid deeper and his thumb stroked her clit, right there, the button of her desire.

"I want to watch you come. I want to see your eyes go wild for me. I want to see the pleasure."

A second finger pushed into her. She was standing on her tip-toes now. Her nails were digging deeply into his arms as she held on tight.

"And that will just be the start," Chance promised her. "Because before I'm done..."

She couldn't be this close to an orgasm. Not with just a few strokes of his hand.

But, oh, that hand of his sure knew just how to touch her.

A moan built in her throat. The muscles in her legs were trembling. He had her pinned against the wall. She only wore her panties and he'd shoved those to the side so he could play with her and stroke her all he wanted.

In and out, those long, strong fingers of his slid. And his thumb...it pushed harder against her clit. Hard and rough.

Just the way she liked things.

"Open your mouth for me..."

Helpless, she did. He kissed her. Thrust his tongue into her mouth even as his fingers drove deep into her once more.

She kissed him frantically, kissed him—

He pulled back.

Her eyes were on him.

His fingers slid out, then pushed into her.

She came, gasping hard with the pleasure and still gazing into his eyes as the wave of release washed over her. Her sex clenched around him, her body shuddered and he smiled.

"So fucking beautiful..."

He made her feel that way.

Even as the climax still shuddered through her, Chance was lifting her higher. Pushing her firmly back against the door and jerking at the opening of his jeans. Yes, yes! He was going to take her right there. She wanted him, all of him and—

A loud, shrieking alarm pierced her haze of passion and pleasure.

At first, the sound of that alarm didn't fully sink in. She blinked and frowned at Chance. He was swearing and pulling away from her. "Smoke detector..." Chance muttered as her feet touched the floor again. "What the hell?"

He whirled away and she scrambled to right her clothes. Her body was still on its after-orgasm high, but an adrenaline rush was bursting through her once again.

Chance had run toward his computer and he was pounding on the keys.

She yanked up her jeans. Twisted and managed to get in her bra and shirt. She'd left her shoes in his bedroom so she made a fast and frantic run in there to grab them, just in case that alarm meant they were going to need a quick exit. When she came huffing back into the room—

"It's on fire."

Gwen froze and looked at Chance.

"The lower floor is on fire. We have to get out of here, now!" He ran toward her and grabbed Gwen's arm.

"I-I don't smell smoke…"

"You wouldn't, not up here, not the way the place is reinforced, but, shit, it's blazing. The alarms should have gone off sooner."

He grabbed a gun from the line of drawers near his door.

"Chance?"

"I don't believe in coincidences. Someone set that fire…and we have to be ready." His fingers locked with hers. "Stay with me."

He wasn't even wearing a shirt. "Chance!"

But he yanked open the door and pulled her outside. That was when the smoke hit her. They were on the second floor and below them, well, Chance just used that area as a garage to tinker with his cars. She knew the guy loved his classic rides. But when she looked over the edge of the stairs, she didn't see his tools. She just saw the flames. Rising and twisting. They were shooting fast across the floor below them.

His hold tightened on her. "We're going for the exit on the right. We'll get down these stairs, we'll stay low, and we'll get out safely."

But there was so much fire.

"Trust me. I won't let anything happen to you."

She did trust him. So Gwen nodded. And they ran down the stairs and straight into the fire.

CHAPTER FOUR

The smoke was billowing, choking him, and Chance could hear Gwen coughing as they made their way through the flames. He should have been alerted to the fire sooner. What the hell had gone wrong?

One minute, he'd been lost in Gwen, and the next...

We're in hell.

They were crouching as they made their way to the exit. The flames were close, but he wasn't about to let Gwen get so much as a blister on her skin. He'd get her out of there, and then he'd find the SOB who'd done this.

They reached the door. With the fire raging so hot, he didn't make the mistake of reaching directly for the doorknob. Screw that. He lifted his foot and kicked at the door. Once. Twice. The door gave way and fresh air rushed inside. He gulped that air greedily even as he cleared a path to exit. When they left that inferno, Chance made damn sure that he went out first. Just in case some unwelcome company was waiting outside — the kind of company that would have started the fire — he wanted to use his body to shield Gwen. He had his gun at the ready and he kept his body as close to Gwen's as possible.

In the distance, he could hear the scream of sirens. When the alarm had finally gone off, he knew the system had sent an instant message to the fire department. The fire fighters wouldn't get there soon enough, though. The place was going up so fast. With all of the oils and paints he kept in his work garage, hell, it was a wonder the building hadn't already blown sky high.

And then the windows shattered as if on perfect fucking cue. Glass flew out. He pushed Gwen behind him and stared at the wreckage.

Someone was going to pay. *Pay.*

***

He smiled when he saw the fury on Chance's face. Oh, but there was no missing that rage. Not with the fire lighting up the scene. It had been simple enough to start that fire. A few Molotov cocktails, a few wires cut…and bam. Instant hell.

Gwen was clinging tightly to Chance. And the guy was holding her just as fiercely. Together, for the moment, but he'd be pulling them apart soon enough.

The fire truck's sirens were growing louder and he could see the lights from the truck in the distance. Like the fire fighters would be able to do anything at that scene. Not now. The fire was too bright. A red and orange beauty that couldn't be controlled.

It just burned.

Some tasks were just so much fun.

***

She'd never been to Chance's office before. *VJS Protection, Inc.*

The gold-lettering at the front had been small. Discrete. The interior went along with that discrete elegance appeal. Leather chairs. A killer view of the city.

When she'd asked Chance what the VJS stood for...he'd explained the letters were initials. V for Valentine, his last name. J for the last name of Jensen, one of his partners, and then S for the last name of his other partner, Devlin Shade.

She knew Chance was catering to upper-end clientele. In that city, the rich and famous were always ready to hire some protection...and Chance was looking to be that protection.

She sat huddled in the leather chair across from his desk. She had ash on her clothes. Soot on her hands. The fire fighters had fought the blaze while she'd just watched — helplessly — as Chance's home went up in flames.

With everything else that had happened that night, she sure didn't buy that fire as being an accident. His home going up in flames hadn't been some terrible coincidence. There was no way her luck was that bad. And if it wasn't coincidence…

Then Chance's home burned because of me. Because some crazy jerk watched us leave my apartment and followed us to Chance's home.

The door opened behind her, the faint sound reaching her ears and causing Gwen to instantly jump to her feet. She whirled for the door. "Chance, I'm so sorry, I—"

Chance wasn't standing there. A tall, handsome blond man was. A man she'd never met before.

He smiled at her. The sight was hardly reassuring. Smiles were *supposed* to be reassuring. But, somehow, when this guy smiled, his face went from handsome…to oddly dangerous.

There is something so wrong with that.

He was a big guy, close to Chance's height and with a similar build, and when the man walked toward her, he used that same easy glide that Chance had.

"Ms. Hawthorne? My name is Lex Jensen and I'm one of Chance's partners here at the agency."

Right. He was the "J" in VJS Protection.

Lex offered his hand to her. His eyes — a dark shade of green, much darker than her own — swept over her.

Gwen knew she was supposed to take his offered hand. Normal people shook hands. It was just that she was feeling pretty far from normal right at that moment. Still, Gwen made herself take his hand. Like Chance, the guy had a rough edge of calluses on his fingers. She knew those calluses — at least Chance's — came from his workout routine. A routine he'd perfected during his time in the military.

Was this guy ex-military, too?

"You've had quite a night," Lex murmured. He didn't let her hand go. "I'm very sorry for what you've been through."

She tugged her hand free. The last thing she wanted to do was get handsy with Chance's friend. Especially after what she and Chance had done at his place. *Done...almost done?* Gwen cleared her throat. "I'm the one who's sorry. Chance lost his home tonight."

"Homes can be replaced. You can't. I'm sure Chance would tell you the same thing."

Gwen thought she caught the faintest edge of an accent in his voice. A hint of the south? Maybe, it was hard to say for certain.

"I was the person Chance sent to do a sweep at your apartment after you left."

The door opened behind him. Chance strode inside. Gwen couldn't help it. She tensed at the sight of him. Like her, ash darkened his clothes. A smear of soot lined his right cheekbone. That man had gotten her out of the fire. He'd risked his life for her. And what had she done?

I brought danger to his door. Hardly a fair exchange.

Lex glanced at Chance, then back at Gwen. "I was just updating Ms. Hawthorne about what I found at her apartment."

"Gwen," she murmured automatically. "Just call me Gwen."

From the corner of her eye, she saw Lex nod. She should look at him, fully, but Gwen was too focused on Chance. And Chance seemed just as focused on her. He strode across the room. Came right to her. He peered down at her with that intent, focused gaze of his. She could still smell smoke, clinging to him. Her hand rose and brushed away the soot on his cheek.

He caught her wrist.

Gwen's lips parted.

"Uh, yeah…" Lex cleared his throat. "I'm still in the room, and I've got intel you both really need to hear."

Chance swore and let her go.

She backed up a step. Seriously, she had to get a grip. Her response to Chance was way off the scales.

"Your hunch was right, Chance," Lex said as he inclined his head toward the other man. "I found bugs in her place. Listening devices. Small cameras. Someone really wanted to keep close tabs on Ms. Hawth—Gwen."

Her stomach knotted. "How long have the cameras been there?" Had someone been watching her for days, weeks? Nausea rose in her throat.

"I can't say for certain."

Damn. *How much did he see?*

But she knew…

Everything.

A light knock sounded at the door.

"Come in," Chance barked.

And another guy pushed open the door and sauntered inside. His hair was as dark as Chance's, but his eyes were a bright blue. He was another big, tall, dangerous kind of guy. The type that—no doubt —made for perfect bodyguard material. His gaze swept the room, and lingered, with a hint of curiosity, on Gwen.

"This is Devlin Shade," Lex said as he quirked a brow. "The last partner in our little business."

"I hardly think your business will stay little for long," Gwen murmured.

Devlin headed toward her. He offered his hand to her, just as Lex had done. She shook his hand, a bit cautiously, and felt the strength in his hold.

"My friends call me Dev," he said as he stared down at her. "I hope you will, too." His voice was quiet.

She managed a faint smile as she pulled her hand back from him.

Dev had a laptop tucked under his right arm. He put the laptop down on Chance's desk and booted it up.

"Dev isn't just brawn," Lex told her. "He's pretty much a tech genius. When I found those little devices tucked away at your place, I called him—"

"And I started working to track the signal on those babies," Dev finished as he leaned over the laptop. "We left them in place and followed the transmission."

Chance moved, a ripple of menace. "Tell me you found the bastard."

"I do believe that we did." Dev glanced up from the screen and smiled. Gwen decided the guys all needed to work on their smiles. Sharks had friendlier grins. "The signal went right back to a little club I think you've heard of…a place called Wicked."

Her gaze flew to Chance at the mention of Wicked. She knew the club and knew he did, too. After all…she'd first met Ethan Barclay in Wicked. The place had opened last spring and become *the* place to be in D.C., provided, of course, that you were looking for a site to party hard.

When she'd been in Wicked that first night, everyone had been catering to her. Later, she'd learned the reason why. Ethan owned the club. He also seemed to own everyone in it. He'd wanted to catch her attention, and he had.

"That sonofabitch," Chance snarled. "I told him to stay away from her."

A chill skated down her spine.

"Guess he didn't heed your warning." Lex's eyes had hardened. "And I'm thinking that means it's time we pay the guy a visit."

A muscle jerked in Chance's jaw. "If that bastard burned my place, if he's the one who's after Gwen, he's getting more than a warning." His eyes glittered. "He's about to face the fight of his life."

Lex nodded.

"Get a tail on him," Chance said. "I don't want the bastard so much as sneezing without me knowing about it."

"Chance…" Gwen touched his arm. "We should call the cops. Give them this evidence. Let them take over the case from here."

All of the men turned equally unreadable gazes on her.

"What?" They didn't need to look at her as if she was crazy. It was a perfectly reasonable request. "You're bodyguards, not vigilantes. You don't need to hunt this man down." She shivered. The last thing she wanted was an encounter like last time. "Just…just let the cops handle it, okay?"

Now the men were exchanging glances. She could practically feel the undercurrents in the room.

"Excuse us a bit, will you?" Chance murmured to the guys.

Lex and Devlin—Dev—hurried toward the door.

Chance braced his legs, cocked his head, and studied her. He didn't speak until the others had cleared the room.

Then, voice low and vibrating with a barely controlled fury, he said, "Someone tried to kill you tonight."

"Chance—"

"That fire was set while you were upstairs with me. Someone cut the alarm. They wanted the blaze to spread until it was too late for us to escape. But that SOB made a mistake. I had a backup system in place, a secondary alarm, and we managed to get out alive."

Her hands twisted in front of her. "I'm so sorry about your home." Her voice sounded as miserable as she felt, and, right then, she couldn't bear to look him in the eyes. If he hadn't come after her that night, if he hadn't followed her from the bar, he'd still have his place. His mementos, his—

"Fuck the home. It never mattered much to me anyway."

Her gaze shot up to him.

"I've had houses in dozens of countries over the years. I've lived in so many places, they all blur together for me." His lips twisted in a grim smile. "You want to know the one place I actually felt comfortable in? Where I felt as if I belonged?"

Gwen nodded.

"With you," he said simply and he gave a hard smile. "You're the closest thing to a real home I've ever had, and I didn't even realize how important you were until you kicked me out of your life."

Breathing was pretty hard right then.

"I never meant to get that close to you. I have a rule...I don't get that close to *anyone*, but you snuck up on me. Slid past my guard, and you got to me." That grim smile vanished. "Then you told me to get the fuck out of your life."

She was actually starting to feel a little dizzy, so Gwen gulped in a deep breath. "You know, it would have been incredibly helpful if you'd told me all of this months before, instead of, you know, dropping this little bombshell on me when it seems as if someone may be trying to kill me."

"My timing is shit."

"It totally is."

"I don't want you to slip away again."

This was the moment. The big moment in her life. The moment that could change her future. Sometimes, you didn't know when these moments were happening, but this time…she knew. "I'm not going anywhere." She'd tried to run from her feelings before, and that had done nothing but brought her trouble. If he wanted them to take a risk together, she was more than game-up for that plan. After all, she'd already spent far too much time loving him in silence. Why not see if they could do more than crash and burn?

His shoulders relaxed. "Good. Good. Lex and I will hit Wicked and fix Ethan."

Um, *fix* him?

"You stay here with Dev and I—"

Gwen knew he'd stopped talking because Chance had noticed her shaking head. "You aren't leaving me behind. This is my life we're talking about. If Ethan is after me, then I think I deserve to be there to find out why he's doing this to me." Besides, should she admit that she felt a whole lot better being close to Chance? She honestly did think of the guy as her guardian angel. No offense to Dev, but Gwen knew nothing about the man.

"Gwen, I don't think…"

"I feel safer with you," she blurted. Well, so much for playing that one close to the vest.

His face softened. She'd never actually seen it do that before. Cute.

"Then you stay with me," he agreed.

Right. Good plan. Another step in that good plan would be...*to call the cops!*

"While Lex was at your place, he picked up some clothes for you. They're in his office. I'll get them sent in here, you can change, and then we'll make plans to hit Wicked."

He turned and headed for the door.

She didn't move. "Are we going to talk about it?"

His hand was reaching for the doorknob, but Chance paused and glanced back at her.

"What almost happened between us," Gwen clarified. *The best orgasm I've had in ages.* And she'd had some fairly good ones over the years. "If it hadn't been for the fire —"

"I'd still be fucking you right now."

Some men would have made a fake boast like that. They would have acted like they could truly fuck that long. *All night.*

But one look in his eyes, and she knew he wasn't lying.

Oh, wow.

"I am going to have you, Gwen. I'm going to have you long and hard, but it won't be here." His lips thinned. "My partners won't be down the hallway, able to hear every sweet sound you make. You and I will be alone, and I'll have you just the way I've fantasized about for far too long."

Her skin was definitely overheating.

He opened the door.

"And I'll have you," she said, her words soft, but she knew he heard them. She saw the sudden tenseness of his shoulders. "The way I've fantasized about for so long. I guess we'll see...we'll see which of us had the better fantasies."

Swearing, he left the room.

Gwen smiled.

But her smile faded a few moments later when she realized...*hell, I have to call my father*. Because if he found out about these attacks before she spoke with him, her dad would freak the hell out. And when Will Hawthorne freaked out, it wasn't a good situation for anyone.

She strode toward Chance's desk. She picked up his phone, and Gwen made the phone call that she dreaded. The line rang once, twice. She glanced at the clock and winced. At this hour, her father would—

"Chance, what the hell is happening?" Her father's voice thundered over the line. "Is my daughter safe?"

She swallowed. "Dad, it's Gwen. And, yes, I'm safe. But there are a few things you need to know."

***

When Chance headed back to his office—with Gwen's change of clothes in tow—he heard the sound of her voice. He'd left the door ajar and he pushed it open. Gwen stood near his desk, and she had the phone to her ear. Her back was turned to Chance as she said, "No, you don't need to worry about me. Dad, look, I told you, Chance is helping me out…"

Fuck me. Her father. He hurried across the room. He hoped Will hadn't done something stupid…like tell Gwen that Chance had been hired to protect her. That would really screw all of his plans.

"Look, Chance is right here," Gwen said quickly. "He can assure you that I am perfectly safe. I've hired him to protect me, so you don't have to worry."

With those words, Chance knew that Will hadn't told Gwen the truth. At least, not yet. He took the phone from Gwen and almost smiled as she mouthed *Thank You!* to him. Obviously, she wasn't enjoying her little chat with her dad. But then, most folks didn't enjoy chats with Will Hawthorne.

Then Gwen took the clothes from him and headed toward his attached bathroom. He didn't speak until the door closed behind her, and then Chance chose his words very carefully, just in case she happened to overhear him. "Gwen is safe. You know her protection is my top priority."

"A fire?" Will nearly yelled in his ear. "Gwen was in a fire? Shit, you should have called me right away! You should have—"

"I was kind of busy getting out of the fire, with Gwen." He kept his gaze on the closed bathroom door. "My partners have been doing recon work. Right now, we think we've got evidence that points to Ethan Barclay."

"I *told* you it was him! I'll destroy that upstart bastard. I'll—"

"I'll be paying him a visit in the next hour. Gwen wants the police brought in, so I'll get in touch with my contact at the department before I head over to Ethan's club. Be assured, I am handling this situation."

"You'd better be," Will snapped right back. "Because if anything happens to Gwen, you're done in this town. Hell, you're done in the whole country."

The guy was confused. His threats had never worked on Chance before, so why would he think they'd work now? Chance didn't speak, and he knew that Will would understand his silence for the *I-don't-give-a-shit* that it was.

"She's all I have," Will mumbled. Those words surprised Chance. "After her mother's death…it was just Gwen. I know half the time she hates me, but I need her. You keep her safe. *Keep. Her. Safe.*"

The guy hung up on him. Big surprise.

But then the bathroom door opened. Gwen stood there, looking so gorgeous she made him ache. Sure, she was just wearing jeans and a t-shirt and her hair was loose around her shoulders, but Gwen wore those clothes better than other women wore expensive gowns. They fit her body perfectly, showing off her curves and making him itch to touch her.

He put the phone back down on his desk. Chance cleared his throat. "I'll change too, then we'll have that chat with Ethan." He sure wasn't looking forward to seeing that bastard. Putting him in jail? Oh, yeah, that part he anticipated.

Gwen nodded.

"I've got some spare clothes, too." He turned away from her. "Just give me a minute…" He was grateful her father hadn't blown his cover, but Chance felt like shit because he was misleading Gwen. He needed to tell her the truth, but he was afraid that if he did, she'd doubt him.

He wanted Gwen's trust. He needed it.

He looked back at her. *Tell her.* But he couldn't. Because she was staring at him with trust filling her bright green eyes, and the last thing he wanted to do was wreck that trust.

She doesn't need to know. But they did need to be clear on one thing. "You told your father you'd hired me to keep you safe."

A light flush stained her cheeks. "Well, yes, I mean, since you have your own bodyguard business and—"

"You're not paying me to keep you safe. *No one* is paying me." He wasn't going to take money from her father and he sure as hell wasn't taking her money. He was protecting her because he needed to know Gwen was safe. If he didn't, Chance would go mad. "I'm doing it because you matter to me."

She seemed to absorb that a moment and then Gwen said, "Just promise, that no matter what happens, you won't get hurt."

He'd been hurt plenty before and he would be again. Lex had even called him an adrenaline junkie once. But then, Lex was the one truly addicted to the high. Chance had already found something he enjoyed more than the rush of danger.

"Chance? Please, I don't want you taking risks for me."

"If not for you, then who?" He smiled at her. "Baby, my life is all about risk. Just ask Lex or Dev. They've got stories that scare even me."

She marched toward him. Caught his hand. Stared up at him with determination stamped on her face. "I'm not talking about stories. I'm talking about the here and now. You say you want me safe? Fine. I want you safe, too. So let's make that happen. Let's both stay safe, let's stay out of any fires…and let's just see what came happen for us. I want a chance to be with you."

And he needed one with her. Needed it, more than he needed anything else.

But he didn't promise her that he wouldn't get hurt. There were already enough lies between them.

CHAPTER FIVE

At night, Wicked was a hotspot teeming with people. The line to gain entrance to the club usually stretched around the block. Music would blare. Laughter would fill the air.

But during the day...especially so early in the day, Wicked was totally different. Deserted. All of the lights were off and no bouncers guarded the doors.

Lex marched toward the doors. He lifted his fist and pounded.

Gwen kept her position near Chance's side. She hadn't seen Ethan in months, not since she'd woken and found him in her bedroom. Chance had come in like a wild fury, and she'd had to pull Chance off the guy. She'd been afraid that Chance would get hauled to jail with Ethan but...

That hadn't happened.

Ethan hadn't been charged with any crime. He'd said that she'd left a key for him.

Total lie.

But she had managed to get a restraining order issued against him. She hadn't seen him since that night, but it seemed as if he'd still been seeing her. Videoing her movements.

The door opened. A tall, broad-shouldered guy with dark red hair glared at them. She recognized the man as Ethan's driver and sometimes bodyguard, Daniel Duvato.

But Daniel's attention wasn't on her. His glare was all for Chance and Lex. "The club is closed, dumb-ass. Come back at midnight." He tried to shove the door closed again.

Lex threw up his hand and stopped the movement. "I'm here to see your boss."

The red-haired guy's eyebrows shot up. "Too bad for you because my boss isn't looking to see anyone right now."

Chance stepped forward. He shoved open that door, sending the redhead stumbling back. "He'll see us," Chance said, his voice strong and commanding. "Go find Ethan and tell him that Chance Valentine is here to see his sorry ass."

Daniel laughed. "You are making one big mistake, asshole. But if you want Ethan as your enemy…" He waved his hand to indicate the empty bar. "Come inside. It'll be your funeral."

"I doubt that," Chance muttered.

Gwen caught sight of Lex's smirk. The guys didn't look intimidated, but her stomach was in knots. Chance's home had been *torched*. This wasn't some alpha guy social call. This was life or death shit. This was scary.

So, yes, maybe she did inch a little closer to Chance. And she did wish that she had a can of pepper spray with her. Or maybe a stun gun or…

"That way," Daniel said, pointing toward the bar. Then his gaze shifted and he finally locked his stare on her. Daniel gave a low whistle. "Oh, but he's gonna want to see you, pretty lady."

Chance growled.

Daniel smiled. "He said you'd come back," he told Gwen. "Sooner or later."

Chance took Gwen's hand and shouldered past the guy. Daniel's mocking laughter followed them.

The bar was familiar to her, unfortunately. When she'd stumbled into Wicked with her friends, she hadn't rushed for the dance floor. She'd gone to the bar, wanting to drink up a little dancing courage. She'd met Ethan at that bar. She'd thought he was just a bartender at first. Later, she'd learned he owned the whole place — and a few other bars in town. He'd had that tall, dark and dangerous vibe and after her rejection from Chance, Ethan had seemed like a temptation she shouldn't pass up.

Too late, she'd learned that the tall, dark, and dangerous label was all too true for him.

Chance strode toward the bar now, and she could see a man standing behind the gleaming, wooden counter top. A man with dark brown hair and broad shoulders. She knew by the cut of his hair, those faint curls, that she was looking at Ethan even before the guy turned around.

But he *did* turn around right then. He had what looked like a glass of whiskey in one hand, and when he saw them heading toward him, Ethan's face tightened with fury. "What. The. Fuck," he snarled. Ethan slammed the glass down on the bar. "The place is closed. Get the hell out!"

She froze, an instinctive reaction, but Chance and Lex just strode forward.

Ethan's eyes glinted with fury. "Didn't you hear me, Valentine?"

Ah, right, like he was going to forget Chance.

"I said get out!" Then Ethan's gold eyes — tiger eyes — locked on Gwen. For an instant, the fury on his face lessened and something else — something that looked a lot like fear — flashed across his face. But in the next instant, all emotion was gone and he was gazing coldly at her. "Gwen."

She shivered.

"Violating your own restraining order, are you, Gwen? I guess some women just can't stay away…"

Chance's hands slammed down on the bar top. "I know what you've done. Did you think no one would find the cameras you set up at Gwen's place?"

Ethan's eyelids flickered. "Cameras?"

"We traced the feed back here. To your place. The cops know, and they'll be here any minute to haul your ass in to the station." Rage growled in each word.

Gwen inched a little closer.

"You torched my home last night," Chance continued, his voice sharpening even more.

"The hell I did!"

"The home can be replaced...but you sonofabitch..." His hands fisted on that bar top. "Gwen was inside."

All of the color drained from Ethan's face. "Wh-what?"

"She could have died!" Chance lunged across that bar, moving faster than a striking snake. He grabbed Ethan's shirt front and jerked the guy close. "Are you just one of those sick bastards that can't let a woman go? Would you rather see her dead than with someone else? She doesn't want you anymore. Get it through your head. Stay the hell away from her!"

Gwen wrapped her arms around her stomach.

Lex was pacing near Ethan's side. "I bet the computer equipment is in the back. This is going to be a slam dunk for the cops."

It looked that way.

Ethan's gaze cut to Gwen. "I didn't do it."

Gwen's lips parted.

"Bullshit," Lex threw out. "The signal tracks back to you. What? Did you get jealous 'cause you thought Gwen was hooking up with someone else? You put a camera in her place so you could watch her. You needed to see her, right. Twenty-four, seven. You—"

"I want to protect you," Ethan said as he gazed at Gwen. His words were rough, raspy. *Just like the voice on the phone?* "Gwen, listen to me. You've got this whole thing wrong!"

"Chance lost..." Gwen stopped and cleared her throat because her voice sounded too weak. "He lost his home, Ethan. The fire was everywhere. Why would you do that? Why?"

Ethan jerked away from Chance's hold. "I didn't! Why the fuck would I want to torch this jerk's home?"

Lex laughed. "Because you thought the jerk in question was screwing Gwen."

She could feel heat staining her cheeks.

Ethan glared at Lex. Then at Chance. "You think I didn't know, even back then, how much you wanted her?" He shook his head. "Gwen was the blind one, not me. I could see how you looked at her. Like the lust was tearing you apart. But *I* got Gwen, not you. She would have stayed with me, if you and her dick of a father hadn't poisoned her against me. Gwen would have stayed—"

Chance leapt over the bar. He just cleared that thing in an instant. He grabbed Ethan and shoved the other guy into the wall of glasses to the right. Chance lifted his fist and drove it into Ethan's face.

"No!" Gwen screamed. Chance couldn't do this, not again. The cops were coming. He'd get hauled to jail with Ethan. She didn't waste time running around the long bar. Gwen climbed right over the thing. Sure, she didn't clear it nearly as gracefully as Chance had, but Gwen managed to stumble over the thing.

Ethan wasn't fighting back, and Chance was gearing up for another swing.

Lex was just watching. *No help at all!*

"No!" Gwen yelled again. She threw herself against Chance and held on tight. "Don't do this! Let the cops take care of him!"

Chance had busted Ethan's lip. She could feel the fury vibrating in Chance's body. The guy needed to back away. If he didn't, she knew this scene was going to end badly.

"Please, Chance," she whispered. "Use some of that famous control of yours."

But Ethan laughed. "Don't you get it, Gwen? He doesn't have control, not when it comes to you."

She sucked in a sharp breath when Chance tensed. "Stop it!" Gwen ordered. And she meant that order for both Ethan and Chance. But she stared hard into Ethan's eyes even as she held tightly to Chance. "It's over. You're not going to hurt me or anyone else that I care about."

Ethan flinched. "I would never hurt you."

Chance dropped his hold on the guy. He stepped back, and his arm curled around Gwen. "Really? Then what the hell were you doing in her bedroom all those months ago? The night you snuck inside? You broke into her place, you—"

"I want to keep you safe, Gwen," Ethan said. He was staring straight at her, and the guy looked sincere. He was a master actor, obviously, so maybe it was no big surprise that she'd fallen so easily for his smooth lines. He'd seemed to care about her. He'd injected just the right amount of sincerity into his voice when they'd been together before...just like he was doing right then.

"I'm safe," she said softly, flatly, "when you're away from me."

His eyes widened. "No!" He tried to reach for her.

Chance shoved him back. "You just don't learn well, do you?"

"Gwen, Gwen, listen to me!" Now Ethan's voice was rising. "I didn't start any fire. And, yes, okay, maybe I did have some cameras set at your place, but it was just so I could watch you! You don't understand the danger you're in. Danger I put you in!"

Chance still had one hand locked around Ethan's shoulder. "Understand this, Gwen isn't for you. You stay away from her. You don't think about her—"

"Gwen!" Ethan's voice was frantic. That emotionless mask was gone. It had splintered right before her eyes. "I can't let it happen again," he shouted.

Again?

"You have to listen to me. I didn't set the fire. It wasn't me!"

Lex's fingers tapped on the bar. "Then who was it?"

Ethan didn't look his way. "You can't trust the people near you. They're working their own agendas. You can trust me. I can keep you safe."

Lex laughed. It was a rough, angry sound. "Wow, you are a ballsy bastard, aren't you? Chance, now I see why you beat the hell out of him before."

She didn't want anyone getting the hell beat out of them. Where were the cops? Chance had put in a call to the police department before they'd left his office.

"I beat the hell out of him," Chance said, his voice grim, "because he broke into Gwen's room in the middle of the night. She'd told him they were done, and the guy wouldn't let go. He snuck into her place. Into my Gwen's bedroom, and he was going to—"

"Your Gwen?" Ethan demanded. "Is that what this is about? You're just trying to get me out of the way so you can finally be with her?" Ethan shoved hard against Chance. A fast, frantic move.

Chance didn't budge.

"She doesn't know what you're really doing, does she?" Ethan snapped as his cheeks reddened. "Because if Gwen knew, she wouldn't be standing with you now, would she? Her father's fucking guard dog. You think I don't know? I've been watching, I've been —"

"Shut up," Chance gritted out.

She could hear other voices then. Rising and falling from the entrance to Wicked. The cops? *Finally.*

"And the cops are here," Lex said, voice mocking. "I'd hoped for a little more one-on-one with this guy first."

Her heart was racing, her breath heaving, and she was really, really glad the cops had arrived.

Before Chance or Ethan started brawling right in front of me.

She grabbed Chance's hand. "Come on," she told him. "Let's go." Then she looked at Ethan. "Stay out of my life." That was the only thing left to say.

She and Chance started walking around the bar. Lex came to her side.

"You can't trust him!" Ethan yelled. "Do you know why he suddenly looked for you again? Months passed, right, and nothing?"

He's been watching me...so Ethan knows everything about my life. That terrible twisting in her stomach just got worse. Yes, she'd felt uncomfortable a few times—out in public, not in her apartment. She'd felt as if someone was out there, watching her.

She'd never imagined that the eyes were on her because someone was watching from *inside* her place. Gwen felt violated. Angry. Scared.

Chance's fingers tightened around hers.

She kept walking. She wasn't going to look back at Ethan. She didn't want to see his lying eyes again. She didn't want—

"He's with you because your father paid him to be!"

She shook her head. That was such bull.

Only...

She happened to be looking right at Lex when Ethan threw out that accusation. And Lex...winced.

Why?

Gwen drew up short.

"Gwen, I'm the one who always wanted you...*you*, just as you are. I didn't give a shit about your father. He wasn't going to stop me from being with you, not like he stopped Chance."

She spun around to fully face Ethan.

"Nothing was going to stop me." Ethan stood there, glaring at Chance. "So this bastard fed you bull about me. He turned you against me."

She could hear the thud of approaching footsteps.

"He fed you lies because Chance wanted you, but he couldn't have you. You were right in front of him, but the guy couldn't touch you. You got tired of all that looking, but not touching, didn't you, Chance? You got tired—"

"I touch plenty now," Chance said, his voice low and cutting.

And Ethan attacked. He snarled and came at Chance with his fists flying.

Chance pushed Gwen back, but Ethan hadn't been aiming for her. Ethan swung and drove his fist at Chance's jaw.

Chance didn't dodge the blow. He could have moved. Could have deflected. Gwen knew what his reflexes were like. Instead, Chance took the hit.

And the cops swarmed. The uniformed men grabbed Ethan and shoved him back.

"That's the man, officers!" Lex shouted helpfully. "Ethan Barclay! He just assaulted my friend and before you arrived, he confessed to putting cameras in Gwen Hawthorne's apartment and—"

"Gwen!" Ethan bellowed. He was fighting against the cops. Twisting. Punching. A bad move. A move designed to get him instantly locked up.

She slanted a glance at Chance. His control was back in place and a tight smile curved his lips.

Chance had wanted Ethan to attack. He'd wanted to push the other man over the edge.

"Gwen, I'm the one keeping you safe!" Ethan was yelling even as the cops started hauling him to the door. A bit of assault against an officer — or three — didn't go over well with them. "You need me! You can't trust Chance! You can't!"

But she did.

Or...*I had.*

Gwen turned and hurried toward the exit. She didn't want to watch Ethan get dragged away in handcuffs. That scene wouldn't provide her with any sense of satisfaction. She'd gone to Wicked that day because she'd thought — somehow — the fear would lessen if she faced off against Ethan.

But the fear hadn't lessened. It had just gotten worse.

She pushed open the door and hurried outside. The cold air actually felt good when it hit her. It was a shock to her system, pushing past her fear and anger.

She stood on the sidewalk a moment. Her hands shaking. Her stomach still knotted.

And she wondered…

Has Chance been playing me?

***

When Gwen ran for the door, Chance immediately started to follow her. Lex grabbed his arm. "No, you see what the cops find in the back. You're the one with the connection to the lead detective. I'll take care of Gwen."

He gave a curt nod and Lex hurried past him.

The cops were there, fighting to subdue Ethan Barclay. It took every bit of Chance's self-control not to jump into the fray but…

Please, don't. Gwen's voice kept replaying through his head. He wasn't going to break down and let the rage consume him again. He needed to be better, for Gwen. He needed her to see him as more than just some hot-headed SOB.

"Well, well…" A woman's voice said from behind him and he turned to see Detective Faith Chestang approaching him. "You always do have a knack for finding trouble, don't you, Chance?"

Faith was in her early thirties, with creamy caramel skin, shrewd eyes, and a killer smile. The woman also had a killer right hook. She'd spent some time on Hawthorne's security detail, so she and Chance had more than a passing acquaintance—and that was why he'd called her. If anyone would back him up at the PD, it would be Faith.

The fact that the woman owed him a few favors had also been one of the reasons he called her. Chance knew—hoped—she'd give him access to the evidence she collected at Wicked.

"Trouble found me this time," he murmured and that wasn't really a lie. "It's like I said on the phone…" He jerked his hand to a now-still Ethan. "The guy was stalking Hawthorne's daughter. He had cameras in her house, and I'm betting if you go to his office in the back…" Chance's gaze slid to the door on the right, the one marked PRIVATE. "I'm betting you'll find video feeds on his computer."

She cocked her head to the right. Her black hair skimmed her jaw. "Is that right, Mr. Barclay? Will I find those files on your computer?"

"I want a lawyer," Ethan said, his face flushed red and his eyes dark with fury. "This is a bullshit case. Chance Valentine is setting me up. He's mad I hooked up with his lady and he's invented this whole scene!"

"So there's nothing on your computer?" Faith asked. She started strolling—as slow and easy as could be, as if she didn't have a care in the world—toward the PRIVATE door. "If that's the case, then it won't matter if I take a peek."

"No!" Ethan shouted. "You need a warrant! You can't go in there!"

"You just assaulted three officers..." Faith said.

The three officers nodded. "Damn straight," one spat. It almost looked as if that officer had broken his nose in the scuffle.

"Getting a warrant isn't going to be hard." Faith smiled that icy smile of hers. One that was both gorgeous and chilling. Chance had seen plenty of men fall before that smile. "So why not save us both some trouble and just confess right now?" She put her hands on her hips. "Have you been stalking Gwen Hawthorne?"

Ethan's jaw jutted up. "I. Want. My. Lawyer."

"And here I didn't think you were the kind of man to hide behind a suit," Faith said, rolling her shoulders. "So much for the word on the street."

Ethan's eyes narrowed.

"But the bigger they are," Faith added, "the harder I take those bastards down." She waved toward the cops. "Get him to the station. He's not going to be stalking anyone today."

He wasn't going to be stalking Gwen ever again.

The cops pushed Ethan toward the door. *So much for getting to search the back office.* At least, for the moment. But Chance wasn't done, not yet.

When the group passed him, Chance eased closer to Ethan. "It's over," Chance said.

Ethan's gaze slid to him. *If looks could kill…*

"I'm not the threat to Gwen," Ethan snapped back, his words a low snarl. "You'll see that. I just hope it's not too late for her when you do."

The guy was still threatening Gwen?

"It's someone else!" Ethan raged.

The cops dragged Ethan toward the door. Chance followed. His steps were slow, certain, and his gaze stayed locked on the SOB. When they exited Wicked, a light flurry of snow fell on them. A police cruiser was parked to the right. Another to the left. Gwen and Lex stood under the building's awning.

The redheaded guy who'd first let them in to Wicked paced a few feet away.

"Daniel!" Ethan yelled at him. "Call my lawyer, get Sophie!"

Daniel nodded.

Then Ethan spotted Gwen. He tried to lunge for her. Chance tensed.

The cops hauled Ethan back and shoved him toward the patrol car.

"Gwen, *Gwen*, I'm not the one hurting you! I wouldn't! I—"

The cops slammed the car door shut. Ethan's yells were blessedly cut off. A few moments later, the patrol car roared away from the curb.

Chance turned to look at Gwen. She was staring back at him. And there was…suspicion…in her gaze.

Hell. He'd been afraid this would happen. Now he had to play this game very, very carefully.

***

"It's not me," Ethan said as he twisted in his seat and looked back through the windshield at Gwen. The snow was falling on her. Chance Valentine was closing in on Gwen. Like a hungry lion. "Don't trust him!" Ethan yelled, but Gwen couldn't hear him.

Gwen thought Chance was one of the good guys out there. She was so wrong. Chance was— hell...

He's as bad as I am.

Chance had walked away from Gwen's life before. What if the guy walked away again? Then what would Gwen do? She'd be out there, on her own, the perfect prey.

He sagged back against the seat. This shit was his fault. He was paying for sins he'd committed too long ago. And things were about to get so much worse. He knew what the cops would find on his computer. He knew exactly how bad the situation would look for him.

But he also knew...he had one fine attorney on retainer. Sophie Sarantos was about to start earning that hefty retainer fee he paid her. She'd

get him out of this, she'd get him away from the
cops…

And then he'd go back to Gwen.

CHAPTER SIX

"Have you been lying to me?"

Okay, so she hadn't meant to just blurt out that question as soon as they were back at Chance's office. But…

They were back in his office. The door was shut. Lex and Dev weren't around. It was just her and Chance. And she was desperate to know the truth.

Chance strode behind his desk. He didn't sit, though. He just stood there. All big and sexy and strong, and he stared at her.

She stared back. Then she marched across the room. Gwen was really happy that her knees didn't knock together when she walked. She thought—hoped—that she looked as cool and in control as he did. She stopped in front of his desk and notched up her chin. Her father did that. He lifted his chin whenever he got pushed into a corner. She'd learned that move from him.

I definitely feel like I'm in a corner. I have to know the truth.

"The guy is fixated on you, Gwen," Chance said, his voice deep and rumbling. "He would have said anything to get himself out of trouble today. He's been videoing you—"

Yes, and that creeped her out plenty. "I'm not talking about Ethan right now. I'm talking about you. About me." She sucked in a deep breath. "Have you been lying to me?"

"I've been back in your life for less than twenty-four hours," Chance said. "Dammit, Gwen, I—"

"Did my father pay you?" She was looking for a reaction. Sharp denial. A guilty flush. Something. Anything.

But his self-control—*damn that self-control!*— held strong. He didn't change expressions at all. His breathing didn't so much as hitch.

"Why did you come looking for me?" Gwen asked. She had to keep pushing him.

"Because you've been in my head for months." His gaze held hers. "I want you...I need you. And I was done waiting."

She wanted those words to be true but... "My father tried to give me a new guard last week. I ditched him." Because she hadn't wanted to live in her father's cage. *Of course, back then, I didn't realize someone had planted cameras in my home!* She might not have been so angry about that extra protection if she had known. "I've pretty much ditched all the guards he's put on me over the years." Her smile felt sad. "Except for you. Did you ever wonder why that was?"

He started to reply.

She waved her hand, stopping him. "It's not because you've got some super awesome spy skills, so don't think that. I've been slipping away from guards since I was six. Since my mom died." *Don't go there. Don't!* "I could have slipped away from you, too, if I'd wanted."

One brow lifted. "I wouldn't be too sure of that."

Cocky. "I am." Gwen had evasion down to an art. "I didn't ditch you because I wanted to be with you." A simple, stark truth. "And my father…he knew how I felt about you. So if he wanted to make sure I had protection, he'd call you. Because he would know that…" *Say it.* "He'd know that I wouldn't be able to turn you away."

Not Chance. The others, yes, but not him.

His eyes had darkened even more with a surge of emotion—but it was emotion she couldn't read.

"You have too many secrets, Chance," Gwen told him, hating that he could be so controlled when she felt so raw from the rip of her emotions. "I don't have any, not from you. I need you to share your secrets with me."

He stared back at her. Just stared.

Fine. She spun on her heel and marched for the door. She wasn't going to bare her soul anymore while he stood there and said nothing. Did nothing. Not while he—

"You father knows how I feel, too."

His words stopped her near the door.

"He knows that I would do anything, *anything* at all, for you."

Hesitant now, Gwen turned back to face him. He was still behind the desk. But his expression wasn't unreadable. There was need on his face. In his eyes. Need, fury.

So much desire.

All for me.

"I've wanted you for a long time, baby. Hell, since the first day I met you. But you were the boss's daughter, and if anyone was hands-off, it was you."

She wanted his hands on her.

She had…since the first day.

"I needed that job, at first. I was looking to build more security contacts, and I knew that job would give me the opportunities I needed. So I worked for your father. I focused on my plans. The dreams I had for my own business. I knew I could make those dreams come alive I if I bided my time. If I did my job for Will."

VJS Protection.

So, right. He'd had his dreams.

She'd had hers. *My dreams were about you, Chance.*

"Then something changed." His voice deepened even more. "I started dreaming about *you*. You got into my head, and I couldn't get you out. I tried to keep a distance between us, but you were smashing right through every wall that I put up. And then that night...shit, that one night when the champagne had been flowing and the snow falling and you—you were in that sexy red dress and you came to me. That damn night—the night I kissed you for the first time..."

"Christmas." No, she hadn't meant to say it, but she had. It had almost been a year before. Christmas Eve. She'd been at her father's home. Chance had been there. He'd just seemed so...lonely. Aloof. She'd learned that he had no family. No one had been waiting at home for him. She'd actually felt his pain, and she'd wanted to comfort him.

But when she'd followed him outside and wrapped her arms around Chance, comfort had soon been the last thing on her mind.

He'd kissed her with wild passion. Kissed her with hot desire. And she'd thought...*finally. Finally, we can be together. Finally, I can have him.*

Then he'd pushed her away.

"I can't do this," she whispered.

"Gwen—"

"Those were your words, when I was offering all of myself to you." Not just her body, but her heart. "And you turned and you walked away from me." She'd just been left standing out on her father's balcony as the snow fell on her. The snow and her tear drops had felt the same as they slid down her cheeks. So cold.

A few months later, she'd walked into Wicked. She'd given into the urge to let go of her emotions. To feel. She'd hooked up with Ethan—

"You stopped coming to your father's. You stopped talking to me." His voice sounded wooden. "You know how some people say they don't even realize what they really have until it's gone? I always thought that line was utter bullshit, but then you slipped away from me. Everything else in my life seemed worthless then. Shit, I used to stay extra hours at your father's business, just hoping I'd catch a glimpse of you. I needed you. I missed you."

She shook her head.

"And when I realized you were more important than anything else, it was too late. You were with Ethan." His jaw hardened. "He wasn't good enough for you. I knew it. I didn't need your father to tell me that. But when Will asked me to dig into the guy's past, I did. And I found the skeletons there."

Shady deals. An ex-fiancée who'd died under mysterious circumstances. Another former lover who swore that Ethan had become obsessed and attacked her…or at least, that was what the police report claimed. The woman had later dropped those charges and seemingly just vanished from the face of the earth. The dark secrets from Ethan's past had kept piling up, and they'd terrified Gwen.

But even before Chance had revealed all of the dirty details of Ethan's past to her, Gwen had already realized she was done with the other man. Her heart had never been with him. She'd been trying to escape the emptiness she felt inside by being with Ethan. But there was no escape.

I could never get away from Chance.

"I was planning to break up with him, even before you came with your evidence." He'd been so cold that day. Just seeing Chance had hurt. And to learn so many painful truths about Ethan. *I suck at choosing lovers.*

Either she picked men who didn't want her…like Chance.

Or she picked men who were psychotically determined to never let her go. Like Ethan?

So screwed.

"I was jealous of him," Chance said.

Her brows pulled together.

"Insanely jealous." Now he walked from behind the desk. His steps were slow. His gaze fierce. "I hated the thought of him touching you. I hated the thought of him being anywhere near you. I wanted him gone from your life long before I found out about his past."

"Chance?"

"Some of the things he said today at Wicked were true. I did think the bastard never should have touched you."

He was closing in on her, and Gwen's feet felt rooted to the spot. She couldn't have moved then, no matter what. But, well, she didn't *want* to leave. Not when he was telling her his secrets.

"I wanted to be the one touching you." He stopped in front of her. And Chance lifted his hand. The back of his fingers slid over her cheek. "I wanted to be the one holding you. The one giving you pleasure. The one giving you everything that you needed. But first, I had to get Ethan out of your life."

Her gaze searched his.

"You broke up with him. Told him to stay away, and I thought I might have a shot with you." His fingers fell away from her. "Then he came after you and...that night...you saw me for the man I truly am."

She grabbed his hand. Her fingers curled around his.

"You told me to stay away, and I did."

Gwen licked lips that had gone too dry. "I was terrified and angry that night. Haven't you ever said anything you didn't mean?"

His gaze fell to her lips. "Yes."

She waited, hardly daring to breathe.

"I can't do this," he whispered.

Those were the words—the four painful words—that had pierced her heart on Christmas Eve.

"Those are the words I didn't mean. Because there was never anything more that I wanted to do...than just to be with you."

She blinked because her eyes were filling with tears. Crazy, ridiculous tears but—

A knock sounded at the door. *No, not now!*

"What is it?" Chance demanded, his voice roughening.

The door opened behind Gwen. She didn't look back. At that moment, she just couldn't take her eyes off Chance.

"Dev and I are going out for some recon work," Lex said. "You and Gwen going to stay here for a while?"

Chance's gaze was on her. "For a while," he agreed.

Her heart nearly leapt from her chest.

"We'll swing by the police station," Lex continued, seemingly oblivious to the tension in the room. Tension that was about to rip Gwen apart. "If the cops have more evidence on Ethan, we'll let you know."

Chance nodded.

A few seconds later, the door closed with a soft click.

Alone.

Chance eased around Gwen and walked toward the door. Frowning, she turned and stared after him—

He locked the door. The lock swung into place with a very solid sounding *snick*. His back was to Gwen. Her gaze slid over his broad shoulders, shoulders that looked a little too tense. His hand flattened against the wood of the door. "I've waited too long for you."

It got even harder for her to breathe and her heartbeat seriously needed to slow down.

"I don't want to make a mistake again. I am so fucking afraid of screwing things up with you."

Big, bad Chance Valentine—afraid? No, that didn't make sense. Gwen shook her head, but then realized he wouldn't see the motion.

"I'm afraid if I don't act now, I'll lose you. You'll walk away or some other bastard will come and take you away." He turned toward her. The hot, hungry look on his face stole the breath that she'd struggled to inhale. "I want you, Gwendolyn Hawthorne. I need you, and, I'm pretty sure that if I don't have you soon, I may just go insane." His lips twisted in a rough smile. "If I'm not already there."

This was happening. Actually happening. The desire on his face wasn't a lie. The need in his voice wasn't some careful trap to lure her in. It was real. He was real.

"I want you, too," Gwen said. That was her truth. Past her fear and the hurt, the desire had always been there. The desire for Chance. To see what they'd have together.

She didn't want him being the lonely man who stood in the shadows, just watching everyone else. A man on guard, always protecting the others, while he stood alone. She moved toward him. Put her hand on his chest, right over his racing heart. It beat just as fast and frantically as her own.

No, she didn't want him to be the man alone. She wanted him to be with her. Always.

So she'd take this risk, and she'd hope that maybe — *please* — he felt some of the same, intense emotions that she did. Not just need. Not just desire.

More.

Love?

Her fingers trembled as they slid down his chest. She opened the buttons on his shirt. Pushed back the material. His chest was so muscled. His abs a perfect six pack. She touched him lightly at first, her fingers grazing over him. She was so nervous because this moment, it mattered. He mattered.

She leaned forward and pressed a kiss right over his heart.

"Gwen, you're going to destroy me."

No, his destruction was the last thing she wanted. His heart? She'd take that. She pushed the shirt all the way off his shoulders and heard the faint rustle when it hit the floor. Then Gwen kissed a path down his chest. There were some faint scars along his rib cage. Slashes near his abs. Battle wounds that made her ache because she hated to think of Chance in danger.

She wanted him to be happy. The guy was always too guarded. She wanted his control gone. She wanted to see him go wild with pleasure. She wanted his laughter. His happiness. She wanted everything that he had to give.

But first…

She would give. The last time, she'd had the pleasure. It was only fair that, this time, he was the one who got his world rocked. Her hand slid down to the top of his jeans.

"Uh, Gwen…"

She glanced up at him. "No one else is in the office, right? Your friends just left."

"But—"

"I want you, and I want you here." So this was where she'd have him. Her fingers pulled open the snap on his jeans, and she slid down the zipper. Chance didn't wear underwear, a sexy bit of information that she'd be remembering for future reference. So his cock sprang toward her. Long and thick and full. So hot.

Her fingers curled around him and she
pumped his length, stroking him from root to tip.
Once. Twice. Three times.

If possible, his cock got even bigger.

"Baby…"

She tipped back her head and met him in an
open-mouthed kiss. Gwen loved the way he
kissed her. Sensually, taking and giving at the
same time until arousal had her aching.

And then she pulled away from him. Staring
into his eyes, she slid to the floor in front of him.

Chance shook his head. "You don't have to —
"

Have to? She *wanted* to taste all of him. He'd
seen her go wild with pleasure. This would be
her turn. Gwen leaned toward him and put her
mouth on his aroused cock. Her lips closed
around the broad tip and she sucked.

"*Fuck.*"

She took him in deeper. Licked and stroked
him. After all, she knew how to use her tongue,
too. His fingers curled around her shoulders as
he held her tightly.

"You're driving me out of my mind."

She wouldn't be satisfied until he *was* out of
his head. Until reason was gone. Control a
memory. She just wanted him to feel.

She swallowed. Sucked him deeper. Pulled
back to run her tongue over the tip of his cock
once more. A light, salty flavor slid over her

tongue and Gwen pressed forward eagerly. She
wanted —

Chance pulled Gwen to her feet. His hold
was rough and his eyes — she'd never seen them
so dark.

"You." The one word was guttural. Sexy. "In
you."

Then he picked her up. Carried her as if she
weighed nothing and that in itself was hot. He
took her back to his desk. Sat her right on top of
that gleaming wood.

"I fantasized about you so much here." He
yanked off her shoes. Tossed them. Pulled down
her jeans and her socks and she had no idea
where her panties had gone but her sex was bare
to him. "Now…I have the real you, not some
dream. *You*."

He jerked up her shirt. Nearly tore her bra
when he yanked it off. Then she was naked on
that desk. Gwen should have felt vulnerable. She
didn't. She felt sensual. She felt…turned on.

"Put your hands on the desk," he ordered.

Her hands slapped down.

He pushed between her legs.

"Can't wait…need you…" But he bent and
took one nipple into his mouth. She gasped at
that contact, loving the feel of his tongue against
her.

Then the head of his cock began to push into
her. *Yes!*

He sucked her breast harder. His hands were locked around her hips. She wanted him to thrust deep—

"Fuck." He pulled back. His breath heaved out. "Condom. Give me one minute, baby." Then he backed away. She wanted to scream with frustration because Gwen wanted him. Right then. They'd both waited long enough.

He came back to her quickly. Kissed her. Positioned his cock between her legs.

When he thrust into her, time seemed to stop. Pleasure rolled through her, and she held on to him as tightly as she could.

He kissed his way down her neck. Lightly rasped her with his teeth. "I've imagined having you a million times, but I never knew…" He withdrew, plunged. "Never knew…it would feel this good."

Her legs lifted and locked around him even as her hands fisted on the table. Time was moving again—at super speed. Her body was wound so tightly and she arched up against him with every thrust. His fingers slid between their bodies. He stroked her clit. Stroked and thrust and she was so close to her orgasm. So close.

Her hands flew off the desk, and she grabbed his shoulders. Her nails dug into him.

This wasn't some gentle bout of love making. It was intense. Hot. Frantic. She couldn't get close enough to him. Couldn't move her hips fast enough. Couldn't take him in deep enough and —

Her climax hit. The pleasure rolled over her like an avalanche, consuming, taking and all she could do was ride out that rushing onslaught of release. The most intense release she'd ever felt. So hot. So good.

And he was right there with her. Gwen felt Chance tense against her. Then he was holding her even tighter as his hips pistoned. "So...fucking...good."

He kissed her again and she tasted his pleasure, just as she knew that he would taste hers. And in the aftermath, he just held her. Wrapped his arms around her and held her so securely against his chest. She could feel his heartbeat slowing against her. At first, his heartbeat had been fast like a racehorse, but its beat was steady now. So reassuring.

She pressed another kiss right over his heart. "I knew it would be like this," Gwen whispered. And she had. She'd looked at him the first day, and she'd needed him. Their chemistry had been electric. She'd wanted him as she'd wanted no other.

Her head tipped back as she stared up at him. His sharp cheekbones were flushed and his eyes glittered.

"I meant for our first time to be in a big-ass bed. I figured I'd do the whole routine.

Champagne. Flowers," he nearly growled the word. "But with you, I just can't hold myself back any longer. I see you, and I want."

Her lips trembled into a smile. "I do the same thing."

He kissed her. Softly. Gently. But then he eased back and a furrow appeared between his brows. "A desk. Shit, did we really just make love for the first time on a desk?" Carefully, he pulled out of her.

She immediately missed him.

Make love. Her heart warmed a little more. "We did," she confirmed, her smile spreading. "And we can make love for a second and third time here, too. Or we can go find that big-ass bed and the champagne and—"

The phone on his desk rang, the shrill cry surprising her and making Gwen jump a bit. She laughed at herself even as Chance glared at the phone.

"It could be your partners," she said as the phone rang again and he didn't answer it. "Maybe they know more about Ethan."

He nodded.

Before he could reach for the phone, her fingers flew out and she hit the speaker button. Because if that *was* Lex or Dev, then she sure wanted to hear their status update on Ethan, too.

Chance's right arm curled around her, and he called out, "This is Valentine, I—"

"I know who the hell you are." The voice of Gwen's father blasted over the line.

For an instant, ice actually seemed to pour over her. She was with her lover, naked — and her father's voice filled the room. Her mouth dropped open in horror.

Chance tried to reach around her, probably aiming to turn off the speaker.

But her father wasn't done talking.

"I'm paying you damn well to keep a twenty-four, seven watch on Gwen," her father snapped. "I expect more updates for my time! Hell, look, I hired you for the job because I knew Gwen wouldn't dodge you the way she does the others. The girl has been hung up on you for too long. We both know she'd let you stay close without giving it a second thought."

The ice that had poured over Gwen got worse. So much worse. She stared at Chance in growing horror.

Ethan had been right. I'm a job for Chance.

"But I deserve updates!" Her father barked. "What happened with Ethan? Did the police arrest that bastard? Did —"

"They arrested him," Gwen said. Her voice came out just as icy as she felt.

Chance's eyes squeezed shut, and he stopped trying to reach for the speaker button.

Gathering her strength, she shoved Chance away from her. Her legs immediately snapped together.

"G-Gwen?" Her father stuttered. He never stuttered. Not William Hawthorne. He made others stutter. He made others fear.

"Chance did his job," she said, her voice sounding as wooden as she felt. "He found me, he stayed close to me, and he stopped the bad guy."

Silence.

Chance's eyes opened. When he stared down at her, his expression looked absolutely tormented.

Good. She felt pretty tormented right then, too. It seemed only fair they should both suffer.

Gwen jumped off the desk. Her knees trembled and she grabbed on to the edge for support. What had felt sexy and wild moments before now felt...wrong. Dirty.

Chance didn't come to find me because he just couldn't stand to be without me for even a moment longer. He came after me because my dad hired him. My dad told him to stay close to me.

She'd asked Chance if her father had hired him. Point blank. He'd kept the truth from her. Gwen bent and snatched up her clothes. She dressed as quickly as she could.

"What's happening?" Her father demanded. "Chance, what the hell—"

"Your timing is shit, Will," Chance said flatly. "I'll call you later."

"Wait, no—"

She saw Chance disconnect the call. She hobbled into her shoes and then unlocked the door as fast as she could.

"Gwen, stop!"

She looked back at him. Chance was grabbing for his jeans. She doubted the guy was going to run after her naked. So she took that moment to make her escape. She didn't stop, didn't pause for longer than a second. She fled.

Because she would be damned if Chance Valentine saw her cry.

CHAPTER SEVEN

Faith Chestang put her hands on her hips. Her gaze slid over Lex, then Dev, and Lex knew the detective was sizing them both up.

"Tell Chance that he's going to owe me even more after this." She gave a firm nod. "Him…and William Hawthorne. Because I know Chance is still on the guy's payroll."

She turned on her heel and headed down the narrow hallway at the police station. Lex hurried to keep up with Faith. "You're wrong about Chance. He's got his own operation now—*we* do." Okay, so that emphasis wasn't exactly subtle, but it wasn't a one-man show. They were partners, and partners watched out for each other. "So I don't know what you *think* you've heard—"

"William Hawthorne told me himself that he'd hired Chance." She paused near the end of the hallway, right beside a shut door. "You're saying Will lied to me?" Anger tightened her face. A whole lot of anger.

Dev cleared his throat. He'd rushed to follow her down the hallway, too. "Why don't we just move to the part where you show us what you found on Ethan's computer...and I'll let Chance know about that increased debt he owes you."

Her eyes sharpened, but she nodded. Then she opened the door.

Lex wasn't particularly surprised to see the computer room that waited. There was a lot of technical equipment in there, but only one other person. A lone tech was inside, hunched over a laptop, typing fast and furiously.

"Hey, Zack, I need you to pull up that video again," Faith said as she sauntered toward him.

The tech, a young guy who looked as if he might be in his early twenties, glanced up. He had a baseball cap on his head and one ear bud slid toward his left ear. He gave a quick nod and tapped again on the machine in front of him.

Dev made his way to Zack's side.

"This guy was watching the pretty lady, a lot," Zack said, his voice slightly nasal. "There are hours of footage here. I mean, seriously, he was watching her for weeks. Maybe even months."

The sonofabitch. Lex knew that Chance would be pissed when he learned that news.

"Pity he's got a high priced lawyer," Faith muttered as she shook her head in disgust. "Because I heard Sophie Sarantos is already working to get the guy out on bail. A man like him doesn't need to be on the streets."

"No, he doesn't…" Zack agreed. He took off his cap. Flipped it around. And leaned over the laptop again. "But he's not the only threat your vic is facing." He pointed to the screen. "Check it out. Right there."

Lex leaned in close to the screen. Dev was already peering hard at it, too. Lex studied the scene on that monitor, then muttered, "Some asshole in a black ski mask is in her room." And that guy's build…his shape…*He looks like the guy I saw at her place the other night.* The bastard who'd slipped away in that van. Lex checked the time stamp on the video. "Hell, that is the guy who gave me the slip the other day! Is it Ethan? Was he putting in more cameras? Was he—"

"That's not one of Ethan's cameras," Zack said.

Dev was still studying the screen.

Zack pointed to the upper left side of the video. "See where the guy is placing the camera? Right there above her bed? The videos that Ethan has—they don't match up to that angle. His cameras were on her doors. Going toward her windows. Hell, almost like he was making sure he had the chance to watch everyone who came in to see her." Zack tapped the screen. "That camera up there is different. It's placed so the man watching her gets an up-close view of your victim. An intimate view. And that feed did *not* transfer to Ethan Barclay's bar."

"What?" Dev demanded. His head jerked to the left and he focused on Zack. "That's not possible. I traced the feeds. They led right back to him! *I* traced them!" Now Dev was sounding all insulted.

"You didn't trace that one," Zack said. "Because that feed didn't go back to the same place."

Oh, hell. *If that feed didn't lead back to Ethan...then who the hell did it lead back to?*

"I'm not wrong," Zack sniffed. Now *he* sounded insulted. "I went to damn MIT. I know computers. I know tech. That feed didn't go back to Ethan's bar—the others did, but that one...hell, maybe he sent it to his home. Maybe we'll find evidence there, but there was nothing related to it on any of the computers that we confiscated at Wicked."

Shit. *Shit.*

Lex looked up and found Faith's gaze on him. "Did you ask Ethan about that feed?" he asked her.

She shrugged. "He's not exactly talking. Not with his lawyer here. They're working on getting the guy back on the streets and any kind of confession from him, well, that's not going to help things, now is it?"

Shit. This case had just gotten one hell of a lot more tangled. Because if Ethan Barclay wasn't the only threat against Gwen…if that jerk hadn't been the only one watching her.

She's still in danger.

***

Chance rushed out of his office building. Big damn surprise…it was snowing again. "Gwen!" The street was decorated for the coming holiday and the twinkling lights lit the scene. He ran right past those lights, sliding a bit on the snow, as he tried to search for Gwen.

He saw her up on the corner. She was standing with her shoulders hunched. *Oh, Christ, please, don't let her be crying.* Gwen's tears tore him apart. "Gwen!" Chance yelled, cupping his hands around his mouth to try and make his call carry to her.

She jerked and looked back. He saw her swipe her hand over her cheek. *Wiping away tears?* When she saw him, Gwen lurched forward. She rushed toward the street.

He was already running after her. "Gwen, stop! Let me explain!" He had to explain this epic fuck-up before Gwen left him.

He heard the growl of an engine. Saw the flash of lights turn on up ahead and then a van was racing down the road.

Gwen was in the middle of the intersection. The sign on the street corner was flashing for her to walk, but she wasn't walking — she was running.

And the van was rushing straight for her.

"Gwen!" Now fear was in his bellow because he was too far away from her. "Gwen, get out of the road! Run, run!"

The van barreled toward her. Chance ran as fast as he could. He needed to get to Gwen. He needed to —

The van roared through the intersection and he saw Gwen fly toward the bank of snow on the sidewalk. She fell into that snow.

The van raced away.

"Gwen!"

Fear stole his breath. He slipped, fell, then hauled ass to her. His whole body was shaking. *Did the van hit her? Did the van —*

She groaned. She was still in the snow.

He reached down to her, and Gwen rolled toward him. Snow fell off her arms and her legs.

"What was that guy's problem?" Gwen mumbled as she brushed the snow off her face. "Didn't he see me? I was right there!"

Chance hauled Gwen to her feet. His shaking hands ran over every inch of her body, searching for an injury.

Gwen can't be hurt. She can't be. I need her. Gwen can't be hurt!

"Stop it!" Gwen swatted at his fingers. "I jumped out of the way. The snow cushioned my fall. I'm fine." She shoved at his chest. "Just let me go."

He held her even tighter. Chance buried his face in the curve of her neck. "Just let me hold you. Give me a minute." A minute to get his fear and fury under control. A minute to realize that he hadn't lost Gwen. She was right there, with him. Safe. Alive.

Her fingers fluttered over his shoulders. "Chance?"

"I couldn't get to you fast enough." His hold was probably crushing her. He should ease up. He just—couldn't. Maybe he needed another minute. Maybe twenty more minutes. "The van was coming right at you. *I couldn't get to you fast enough.*"

She pushed against his shoulders. Finally, Chance managed to ease back, just a few inches. Her expression was worried. "I'm okay," Gwen said softly. "It was just an accident, I'm—"

His phone rang, vibrating in his pocket.

Gwen's jaw tightened. "That had so better not be my father again."

Chance kept one arm around Gwen while he pulled out his phone. His gaze swept the area. The van was long gone.

That van had been familiar. I saw it before, back at —

"We've got a problem," Lex said when Chance put the phone to his ear. "A big damn one. You need to get down to the police station with Gwen because it sure looks like Ethan may not be the only threat facing your lady."

"Yeah, yeah, I got that part already." Because that van—that dark van—it had been the same one he'd seen the other night at Gwen's place. He knew that make and model. The guy had just tried to run her down. *He tried to kill Gwen.* "We're on the way." He put the phone back into his pocket.

"Chance?" Gwen stared up at him.

Oh, hell, but he hated to do this… "Baby, that wasn't some distracted driver." He went back into the road. Pointed to the marks that were so easy to see in the falling snow. "The driver was waiting for his moment to attack. When he saw you, when you made a good target, he came right at you. He accelerated and he swerved to try and hit you. Not to avoid you." The marks on the road told a clear story.

Gwen's arms wrapped around her stomach. "That guy wanted to kill me?"

Kill her…or, at the very least, hurt her. Badly.

"Why? What have I done? Is Ethan doing this? Did he hire whoever was driving that van?" Now she looked down the empty road. She shivered. "I want this over."

So did he. "We need to get to the police station." There was a camera positioned right above the intersection. Faith would get them access to that camera. They'd find that bastard.

And I will stop you. Because you aren't going to take Gwen from me.

***

At the police station, Gwen stared through the one-way mirror into the interrogation room. Ethan was seated at the table, and he seemed to be staring right back at her.

"He can't see you," the detective told her. Faith. The detective's name was Faith Chestang. She'd been waiting when Gwen arrived at the station. Faith had worked for Gwen's father years before, and Gwen had been glad to see a familiar face at the PD. "He knows someone is out here, of course," Faith added, "but the guy has no idea it's you."

One of Ethan's wrists was handcuffed to the table.

"Why is he doing this?" The *why* was driving Gwen crazy. "We broke up. People do that all the time. They break up, and then they move the hell on." They didn't put cameras inside the homes of their exes. They didn't—jeez, what had he done? Hire someone to mow her down in that van?

"You know his ex-fiancée died in a car crash." Faith's voice had turned musing.

Gwen didn't look away from Ethan. It was hard to think that she'd once had sex with a man who now wanted her dead.

"I did some digging on that incident," Faith said. "And I'm not so sure it was an accident."

Her words pulled Gwen's gaze off Ethan. "What?"

"She was driving a brand new car. Her brakes shouldn't have gone out, not without some help. If we still had the car, I'd get my techs to go over it...because I'd lay odds we might find some new evidence in that case."

Gwen rubbed her aching temple.

"Men like this...obsessive stalkers...they don't just suddenly develop the condition overnight. Ethan Barclay has done this before, in other relationships. I'd bet my badge on it."

And she understood why the detective had brought up Ethan's ex-fiancée. "You think he killed before."

"Some men have a hard time taking 'no' for an answer." Faith stepped closer and stared through the glass. A badge was clipped to her right hip and a gun holster was on her left. "His lawyer won't let him talk to me. Not to any cop. She's pulling every string she's got so the guy can get out of here as fast as possible." Faith glanced over at Gwen. "I'm going to be very honest with

you. It doesn't matter how much power Will has
in this town, the judge can't keep Ethan locked
up forever. He will get out on bail. And when he
does, you need to be prepared." There was a dark
warning in Faith's eyes. "He's locked on you, and
I don't see him just turning away now."

He's going to come after me again. And to think,
she'd tried to push off her father's protection.
"My dad was right all along."

"Yeah, well, when you tell him that, Will is
going to be even harder to live with."

Faith kept speaking so easily about Gwen's
father. Suspicion nagged at Gwen. She'd
wondered about the two of them before...

Once again, Faith looked through the one-
way mirror. "Chance is going over those videos
with Lex and Dev. If he was in here with us now,
Chance would never let you do what I'm about to
suggest."

Gwen's shoulders stiffened. "He doesn't 'let'
me do anything. I make my own decisions and
choices." The guy could rage all he wanted. She
wasn't backing down for anyone. *My life. My way.*

"Like I said...Ethan in there won't talk to a
cop, but you aren't exactly a cop."

Gwen's palms started to sweat.

"You want to find out if Ethan hired the
driver of that van? Then why don't you go in
there and ask him. He's cuffed, and I'll make sure
an officer stays in the room with you at all times."

Faith glanced over at Gwen. "If he's as hooked on you as I think, he'll want to talk to you. He'll want to tell you what's been happening. Want to convince you that he's not the monster you think he is." Her expression tightened. "But he *is* a monster, never forget that."

Right. Gwen slowly blew out a breath. "I'm going in." Because it was her decision. Her life. Chance and Gwen's father had already played her enough. She wanted this nightmare to end, and the man sitting cuffed in that little room — he could end it for her. Ethan could give her the name of the man who'd been in that van. Man — or men. Whoever it was that Ethan had hired to terrorize her.

Then she could walk away. Start putting the pieces of her life back together.

"I was hoping you'd say that," Faith murmured. She turned and headed for the hallway that led into interrogation. "Stay cool and stay in control," Faith advised her. "He's the one in cuffs. He can't hurt you anymore."

Gwen followed, her steps a bit slower. The creak of the interrogation room door opening sounded far too loud to her ears.

He can't hurt you anymore.

Ethan looked up when the door opened. The instant he saw Gwen, he jumped to his feet. "Gwen! Finally! I've been telling my lawyer that I needed to talk to you —"

He had? Well, no wonder Faith had pushed for this little one-on-one.

"Five minutes," Faith said, her voice flat. "That's all the time you get with her, Barclay."

Ah, so Faith was acting as if she didn't want this little meeting. Clever. Another way to manipulate Ethan. Gwen was all for manipulating the guy. Especially considering how much the man had been tormenting her.

Then Faith turned on her heel and left the room. The door closed behind the detective. Goosebumps immediately rose on Gwen's arms. It was oddly cold in that little room.

A uniformed officer watched from the corner.

"I wouldn't hurt you," Ethan said. His voice seemed to drip with sincerity. Like she'd be buying his lines anytime ever again. "I hope you know that, Gwen. No, I *need* you to know that."

She just glared at him. "Sit back down, Ethan." She didn't want the guy towering over her.

His eyes crinkled faintly at the corners, as if he were trying to figure her out, but he slowly sat down. She didn't. One thing she'd learned from her father's business dealings…when you were facing an adversary, you needed to stay in a position of strength. Sure, her standing while Ethan was sitting wasn't exactly much of a power play, but it still made her feel better.

"I should have explained things sooner," Ethan said, his voice a bit halting. "But I didn't think you'd believe me. And I thought...hell, maybe it wouldn't happen with you. Maybe you'd be safe. You'd left me, after all...so maybe—"

She lifted her hand, stopping him. "What are you talking about?" The guy's words were so jumbled that she could barely understand him.

His lips thinned. "You're being stalked."

She almost laughed. "I know. By you."

"No." Ethan shook his head. "I was protecting you. That's why I had cameras at your place. You'd cut me out of your life, got that restraining order. I couldn't get close, but I had to make sure he didn't come for you, too."

Her chest was aching. "He?" She needed to keep him talking. She might want to turn and run away, but the key to her life—it was in this room. Either Ethan had hired someone to terrorize her while he was locked up in jail or—

"He's done it before. More than once. He takes away what I care about, and I don't even know why."

He takes away what I care about. Not what...who? "Your ex-fiancée."

His fist slammed into the table. "Jena wasn't my ex! She *was* my fiancée! We were still planning to get married then..." His words trailed away as his shoulders hunched.

"Then you killed her."

His head whipped up. "The hell I did."

"Someone tampered with her brakes." At least, that was Faith's theory, and Gwen was willing to run with it right then, just to see Ethan's reaction. "What happened? Did she cut you out of her life, too? And you got pissed at her, just as you did with me?" Damn him, she didn't deserve this. "I didn't love you, Ethan. We were going to break up even before Chance and my father told me about your past."

He swallowed, his Adam's apple bobbing faintly. "I know you didn't love me. You were too hung up on Chance to ever love me." His head tilted to the right. "Do you love him, Gwen? Is he the one in your heart?"

She wasn't about to tell him anything about her heart. She turned, acting as if she were heading for the door. "You don't have anything useful to say—"

"I didn't touch Jena's brakes. And I never laid a hand on my ex-girlfriend Marjorie, either."

Marjorie. Chance had showed her a picture of Marjorie's battered face. That picture had sickened her. "I saw the police report. Marjorie went to the cops. She told them you attacked her."

"She *withdrew* those charges because she realized what was happening."

Gwen turned around to face him. "Where is Marjorie?"

Because neither Chance nor Gwen's father had been able to find the woman.

"She's safe." His gaze cut toward the mirror on the nearby wall. The mirror that tossed back their reflections instead of showing them just who was watching in that observation room. Gwen had no doubt that Faith was out there right then.

"Safe?" A fist squeezed her heart. "Tell me she's not dead."

His gaze flew back to her. "I am not a killer, dammit! I knew her attacker would strike again, so I got Marjorie the hell out of here. I sent her out of the country. Gave her enough money to start fresh. When I say she's safe…" He exhaled on a ragged breath. "I don't mean she's lying in a grave someplace. I mean that she's far away and the bastard can't hurt her again."

Gwen found herself inching a little closer to him. "What bastard?"

"If I knew his identity, I would have stopped him by now." He looked down at the handcuffs. "Hell, maybe I am a killer. Because of what he did to Jena, to Marjorie…to you…I think I could murder him."

The drumming of her heartbeat filled her ears. "Marjorie must have seen the man who attacked her."

"He was wearing a black ski mask."

Oh, shit. *Just like the man who attacked me.*

"She thought it was me because we'd fought hours before. And when the guy slipped into her place, he used a key. He didn't force his way inside. He just unlocked the back door." Pain flashed across his face. "*I* had a key. He was my height. My build. He knew how to walk through her house without so much as making the wooden floor creak. So she thought it was me."

Yes, Gwen could sure see where the woman would make that leap. *Especially since I woke up one night and found Ethan in my bedroom…*

"But it wasn't me. I would never hurt her. Or you." He stared into Gwen's eyes. His expression was stark, so desperate. "My mother was abused. My bastard of a father made it his goal to terrorize her. I would *never* be like him."

That sincerity was there again. Shining in his eyes. Nearly dripping from his words.

Gwen shook her head. "I want proof."

"Check my video feeds—the jerk was at your house! I saw him…he was putting a camera into your bedroom. I rushed over there to find you, but you were already gone."

She'd gone to Chance's house…and the place had been torched.

"Why did he go after Jena?" Gwen asked. "Why Marjorie? Why me?" Nothing he said made sense to her. *That's because Ethan doesn't make sense…he's crazy!* He had to be, right? After all he'd done?

"He targeted you — hell, he did it because the three of you weren't casual fucks." His uncuffed hand shoved through his already tousled hair. "Because he thought I could care about you…about Marjorie. He thought I'd care about you and Marjorie the way I cared for Jena, and that sick freak, he won't let me be happy." His eyes had gone hot with fury. "He called me once. Told me that. His voice was low, rasping, and he told me that I'd never be happy. He said he'd see to it…I didn't know what he meant, not then. Not until I found myself in a morgue, identifying Jena's body."

Dear God. If his story was true…

Gwen didn't have a stalker. Well…she had *Ethan's* stalker. The attacks weren't about her at all. "You and I aren't together. It doesn't make sense for him to come after me…"

He was staring at the handcuff again. "It had been so long since Marjorie. I thought…I stupidly thought the guy was gone. I hoped he was dead." His shoulders rolled back. He sighed and confessed, "I made a mistake. I bought you a ring."

***

"I bought you a ring…"

Chance wanted to punch right through the glass. Gwen was staring at Ethan in shock, and a faint tremble swept over her.

"The guy was gonna marry Gwen?" Lex asked from Chance's side. Then the guy gave a low whistle. "Hell, I did *not* know that."

Chance turned his head and glared at his partner.

"As twisted up as you are about her…man, you were just going to let that happen?" Lex pushed.

No fucking way. "I didn't know."

"Well, you should—"

"Shut the hell up," Faith snapped. "I'm trying to hear."

And Chance was trying to keep his sanity. He looked back through the glass. "Ethan is playing her. Gwen is far too trusting."

"Right…" Lex drawled, but his voice was softer now. "Far too trusting. Like the time when she believed you came after her out of some unrequited love, and not because her father offered to throw a big wad of cash at us."

Why was Lex pushing him? "The money didn't matter to me. You know that."

"Did the woman?"

"Yes," he gritted out.

Gwen mattered. She mattered more to him than anything else.

Now how the hell was he supposed to prove that to her? He'd fucked up, and he wasn't sure if Gwen would give him a chance to get close again.

One moment of paradise…and then Chance had been plunged straight into hell.

CHAPTER EIGHT

Gwen grabbed the back of the chair. "What? A ring? We'd only dated a few weeks." She'd kept seeing him, hoping she'd feel more for him. Feel that deep connection that had clicked for her with Chance. But…she'd never clicked with Ethan.

"It was a token of my affection. Not a marriage proposal." His lips twisted. "But that was a screw-up. He was watching. He knew I was getting too close to you. He must have known…right after we broke up, that's when I got the first picture."

Gwen licked her lips. "What picture?"

He stared up at her. "Your picture. It was you, working at the gallery. You were in paint-stained jeans and you had your hair pulled back in a pony-tail. It was a close shot, one that someone must have snapped with a phone…it looked as if the guy was only a few feet away from you." His twisted smile was gone. "I got a message with that photo. A text that said…NEVER HAPPY. I knew what the fuck he was saying. I knew he was coming after you, and that's when I snuck into your place. I was trying to come and warn you about him—"

But he'd nearly scared her to death. "You didn't tell me."

His gaze shot to the mirror. "That's because Chance didn't let me. It's hard to talk when a jealous rival is shoving his fist into your face."

No. Gwen shook her head. "You had plenty of opportunities. You could have come to me later. Told me—"

"You took out a restraining order on me! I didn't have a lot of options. I was trying to keep you safe the only way I knew how." His breath heaved out. "Don't believe me? I told your father. I asked him to keep guards on you. He knows what's been happening."

What?

"This is my fault," Ethan continued doggedly. "I brought you into this guy's sights, and now he's locked on you. You have to get out of the country, you have to get away, just like Marjorie did."

She was supposed to run? To leave her family and her friends behind? To leave the gallery she'd built from the ground up?

Gwen glanced at the little clock on the wall. It was right above the uniformed cop's head. That cop hadn't so much as twitched while she'd been in the interrogation room. "I think your five minutes are up."

"You believe me, don't you?"

She didn't answer. "Do you know anyone who drives a black van?" Gwen asked as her gaze pinned Ethan.

He shook his head.

"That van nearly ran me over less than an hour ago. That same van was at my apartment when a man in a black ski mask raced away from the building. That man tackled me." She considered the memory. "He was your height, your build."

"It *wasn't* me."

"Then who was it? Who hates you this much?"

"Hate? Well, I'm sure Chance Valentine hates me plenty."

"It's not Chance." Anger snapped in her words. He hadn't just gone there.

"I know that." Ethan's jaw worked. "But Chance is pissed because I was with you. Chance thinks you're his. Maybe...hell, this all started with Jena. Maybe she had someone in her life who thought she didn't belong with me...someone who thought of her as *his*. And when Jena hooked up with me, that's when his rage exploded. He took Jena. He tried to take Marjorie and now—"

The door to the interrogation room flew open. Gwen turned and saw Chance filling the doorway.

"No one is taking Gwen away." His voice was guttural.

He was wrong on that. "Gwen is taking herself away," she muttered. Because she had to think. She had to figure out who was telling her the truth.

If anyone was.

She pushed past Chance and stormed into the hallway. But she'd only taken a few steps when she stopped.

Faith was in the hallway. Lex and Devlin were there.

And so was her father.

***

"I don't remember agreeing to talk with you," Ethan said as his angry stare narrowed on Chance.

Chance shrugged. "You don't have to talk. Just listen." His fingers were loose at his sides. With extreme effort, he kept his control in place. This wasn't the time for rage and hate. This was the time to protect Gwen. "She almost died tonight. That van came far too close to her. *I* wasn't close enough to save her —"

Ethan jumped to his feet. "Then you weren't doing your job!"

Back to that, were they? "You *did* go to Will." When it came to lies and deception, he was an expert. Gwen...she was too trusting, but he fucking loved that about her. He loved that she had hope. Loved that she believed in people.

Fuck me...I just love her.

He was the cynical one. The one who didn't believe in anything or anyone...but her.

I believe in Gwen. Always will.

"You convinced Will that there was a threat to Gwen, and he came to me."

Ethan's lips clamped together.

"I have to know who I'm fighting," Chance snarled. "You said it started with Jena...but you never had proof of that, right? You've already torn into her past." He'd bet on it. "But you didn't find any scorned lovers."

Ethan gave a quick, negative shake of his head.

"Then maybe it didn't start with her. Maybe there was someone else, *before* her. I need names, man. Write down a list of your lovers. I don't care if it was the freaking first girl you kissed when you were thirteen, I need to know." Because the women were the key. The women were being attacked, not Ethan.

He could hear voices coming from the hallway. "Get me that damn list." He spun for the door. He needed to talk with Gwen—

"Promise you'll keep her safe."

He looked back.

"If he tried to kill her tonight…again after the fire at your place…then he's going to attack again. That's how it was with Jena."

The guy had said he wouldn't talk with Chance, but he was sure talking plenty right then.

"Some creep nearly mowed her down…she thought it was just some drunk driver. So did I." His voice roughened. "I wish I'd realized what the hell was happening sooner." Ethan's shoulders sagged. "Now I know…he was hunting her. Just like he's hunting Gwen. And he's not going to stop, not until she's dead."

"That's not happening." There was no way Chance would let that happen.

"Protect her."

Fucking always.

He hurried out of that interrogation room. He saw another cop rush in even as Chance left. But Chance wasn't focusing on the cop. There was too much action in the hallway.

Mostly because Will Hawthorne was there.

Will was glaring at Lex—and at Dev. "I paid your team to guard my daughter! She's supposed to be safe, and not having some cozy little chat with the bastard who's been stalking her!" With each word, his voice rose more.

Chance's eyes narrowed as he marched forward. "You want to be pissed with someone," he said flatly, "you be pissed with me."

Gwen wasn't looking at him.

Faith stepped forward. "*I'm* the one who asked Gwen to go in there, Will."

Will's gaze slanted toward her. Huh. Was it Chance's imagination or had Will's face just softened as he stared at the detective?

But in the next instant, rage was back in place on Will's visage. His attention snapped back to his daughter. "Gwen, come on, we're leaving. We'll go back to my estate where I know you'll be safe."

He turned on his heel. The guy had guards with him—men Chance had once supervised when he'd worked for the mogul. The guards inclined their heads toward Chance—a brief gesture of acknowledgement—then they closed in near Will.

But Gwen didn't move.

It took Will a few moments to realize that she wasn't following him.

When he did, Will glanced back, frowning. "Gwen?"

"Did Ethan come to you and tell you that I was in danger?"

Will's lips parted in quick surprise. His eyelids flickered—a little jerk.

Sonofabitch—he had.

Gwen must have caught the telling movements because she nodded. "That's when you started insisting that I needed all the bodyguards, right? You thought Ethan might be telling the truth…you thought someone might be after me."

Will hurried to Gwen's side. "Someone *is* after you!" He pointed to the interrogation room. "Ethan Barclay! The man obviously has psychotic issues—he's fixated on you and—"

"You should have told me, immediately, what he said. Instead, you tried to manipulate me." Her voice was so cold. So unlike Gwen's normal warm tone. Her gaze flickered toward Chance. "You both did."

He hated for her to look at him that way. His back teeth ground together as Chance said, "I just thought Barclay was a suspect. I didn't realize he'd told your father someone else was after you." That bit of information would have been helpful to know.

Will reached for Gwen's hand. "Barclay is just trying to confuse you. There is no one else. He wants you to soften toward him. Hell, maybe he thinks you'll drop the charges against him or something if you buy into his wild story. Doesn't matter, though. The truth is…Ethan Barclay is the man behind the attacks. He's—"

"When a black van tried to run me down tonight, Ethan was in jail." She tugged her hand free of his.

"One of his flunkies!" Will instantly railed. "Someone he hired to make himself look innocent!"

Dev and Lex shared a long look.

"Maybe," Gwen allowed. "Maybe not." Then she walked past her father.

Will stood there a moment, looking lost. Strange, for him. But he rallied quickly and motioned for his guards to follow Gwen. "We're going home," he announced as his stare shifted back to Faith. *And it did soften a bit.* So the rumors about those two must be true. Interesting.

"Keep me updated on this case," Will told Faith. "I want to know everything that happens with Ethan."

She nodded.

"I'm not going home with you." Gwen glanced over her shoulder. "I'm tired of being manipulated…" Her gaze swept over them all. Lingered on Chance. "…by everyone."

Fuck.

"I'll check in to a safe hotel. One with plenty of security cameras and a respectable staff. I'll be more than protected for the night." She straightened her shoulders. "Faith, you have my cell number. Just call if you need me."

She was leaving them all.

"No!" Will snapped. "You need—"

Gwen's smile was sad. "I know what I need, and it's to be left alone. Before I seriously explode on you." Her smile trembled, then vanished. "And I know what you need, too, Dad. You need to stop trying to control everyone and everything. Mom's death wasn't your fault. Even if you'd had a dozen guards on her...bad things still happen. You can't protect everyone, not all of the time."

Will backed up a step. "You—"

"She was robbed in broad daylight, Dad. Mugged and stabbed. And I was in the car. I saw it all."

Will had backed up a bit more, but Chance found himself rushing toward Gwen. He knew the story about her mother, but there was such pain in Gwen's voice. He just wanted to hold her and take that pain away.

But she stiffened when he approached, and Chance stilled.

"I saw that the world wasn't always a good place when I was six. It's filled with darkness and danger. But that darkness...it's just part of life. You can't remove it completely. It's just not possible." Her breath was ragged. "You can't lock up the people you care about—"

"I just want to protect you," her father rasped.

"You can't lock them up," she continued with a sad shake of her head, "because that's no way to live." Tears glistened in her eyes. "You can't surround a person with guards every second and you can't...you can't buy lovers. *You can't control everything for them!*" Her hand swiped over her cheek, wiping away a tear that had fallen. "No one can be safe every moment, and when you fill someone's world with guards...it just makes them...it makes *me* feel like I'm suffocating." Then she turned and headed for the door. She didn't run. Just walked with slow and certain steps.

"Follow her," Will ordered his guards.

When they rushed forward, Chance lifted his arm, barring their way. "Stay the fuck away from her."

The men immediately stepped back.

"I gave you an order!" Will marched toward Chance. "I'm the one who pays them, and I'm—"

"You're going to drive her away completely." Chance lowered his voice. "She'll leave you. She'll leave me. For good. That's not what either of us wants."

Fear flickered in Will's eyes. "I just want her safe."

Because Gwen had been right, and Chance knew it. Will blamed himself for the death of

Gwen's mother. He'd been away on business. Denise had been out, shopping with Gwen. And when she'd died in the street, Will had been over two thousand miles away.

Dev—who'd been slumped against the wall on the right, avidly watching the scene—pushed up and sauntered down the hallway, following quietly in Gwen's wake.

Lex just kept watching the action unfold.

"I'm going to ruin you," Will said, the fear still in his eyes, but fury appearing now. "This is your fault. If anything happens to her—"

"Save your threats. I don't give a shit about them."

Will's lips snapped together.

"The only thing I care about is Gwen. And I will *not* do anything to hurt her. No more secrets. No more lies. Not ever." He'd do anything necessary to prove himself to Gwen. Because she mattered. Plain and simple.

Will's heavy brows lowered as the older man seemed to consider him. "When did my daughter come to mean so much to you?"

From the minute I met her. But that was for him to tell Gwen. "Keep your guards back. Gwen told you what she wanted, and, from now on, the only thing I care about…is giving Gwen what she wants."

"I care about keeping her safe! I care about finding the guy who nearly ran down my daughter! I care—"

Faith cleared her throat. "We've got patrols looking for the van now. We caught the vehicle on one of the traffic cams. Got the make and model, no tag, but we're looking for the guy. Every cop in the city will be searching for the perp. He won't get away."

No, he wouldn't.

Chance marched down the hallway. Gwen was long gone, and so was Dev.

"Are you going after my daughter?" Will called after him. "Are you going to protect her? Are you going—"

"I'm going to apologize to her, and then I'll see what the fuck happens after that." He didn't have anything else to say, not to Will, anyway.

But he sure had plenty that he needed to tell Gwen.

***

Will's hands were fisted at his sides. Gwen had left, and Chance had just basically told him to screw off. "James and Harvey," he said to his guards, "I need you to—"

"I'd think carefully about that," the blond-haired man to the right said. Lex. Lex Jensen. He knew the guy…Will had researched him as soon as he'd learned Lex and Devlin Shade were in business with Chance. Lex had served in the military with Chance, but after his tour had ended, Lex had kept working in the Middle East and in Russia as a mercenary. A lot of his past had been covered in secrecy, and even Will's government contacts hadn't been able to provide him with many details about the man.

Will's gaze swept over the younger guy, sizing him up.

Lex gave him a wide grin. "I mean sure, if you want to piss off your daughter and ruin the last hope of a relationship that you have with her, go right ahead. But if you actually care about the woman…" His shoulders pushed away from the wall as he straightened. "Then maybe you should put some trust in Chance. Because I know for a fact, that man would give his life to protect Gwen."

Will knew that, too. Actually, he'd counted on it. He'd known Gwen wouldn't turn Chance away when he came calling…because Gwen cared about Chance.

And as for Chance…Will had known he was the perfect guard for her…*because Chance more than cares for Gwen. The guy loves her…and he doesn't even realize it.*

Or maybe, Chance did. Maybe he'd finally wised up. Judging from the look that had been in

Chance's eyes, Will thought the guy had finally figured things out. *Just in time.*

"Will doesn't trust easily," Faith said as she approached them.

He nearly winced at her words, and Will couldn't help but cast a guilty look her way. Dammit, in spite of the nightmare surrounding him, he still noticed that Faith looked beautiful.

She always did.

"He likes to use people," Faith continued. "That's sort of Will's thing. His specialty."

He did wince then.

"He uses them. He doesn't trust them."

So she was *definitely* still mad at him. Right. He made a mental note to send her more diamonds. But the diamonds hadn't exactly worked in the past. Not with her. Faith had never given a flying shit about his money. She wanted something far more important from him.

She sauntered forward. Her hand was close to her holster. A little too close for his peace of mind.

"Isn't that right?" Faith asked him. Her dark eyes gleamed with a hundred emotions. "Trust isn't an option for you."

As he stared at her, Will couldn't speak.

"Maybe it should be," Faith said. "Maybe you should trust Chance this one time. I saw the emotion in his eyes, just the same as you did. Do you really think he would do anything to put Gwen at risk?"

No, he didn't. So he didn't give the order for his men to rush after Gwen. He knew Chance would protect her from any threat. But he also knew…

Chance…you can hurt her. Gwen's vulnerable to you.

If Chance screwed this up with Gwen, Will would make him pay.

CHAPTER NINE

Chance jumped out of the taxi and tossed his cash to the driver. He yanked up his collar and a soft plume of chilled air appeared above his mouth as he stared up at the gleaming lights of the hotel. Just blocks from 1600 Pennsylvania Avenue, Gwen had chosen one of the swankest hotels in the city.

And one with top-notch security.

He headed for the entrance. Two doormen were there, their assessing gazes sweeping over him as he walked inside. Once in the lobby, he spied the security guard near the elevator. Chance glimpsed another guard watching near the check-in desk.

"You got here faster than I thought," Dev murmured as he strolled to Chance's side. "Someone was hauling ass, huh?"

Yeah, he had been. "Did Gwen see you tailing her?"

Dev stroked his chin. "Let's see…before she boarded the elevator—the one that only takes you up to concierge level if you have the special key card for access — she *did* turn in my direction and flip me the bird."

Chance's brows rose. His lips twitched.

"So, yes, I'd say it's safe to assume that Gwen caught sight of me."

Chance ran a hand through his hair. "Did you get her room number?"

"1608. I figured you'd be requesting room 1610…the one right beside her."

Damn straight, he would be.

"I didn't see anyone else tailing us to the hotel. So either the guy is good, really good, or the APB that Faith put out on the van has him in hiding for the moment. I'll stick around though," Dev said, "and keep my eyes peeled. Extra protection can't hurt, right?"

No, it sure couldn't. Chance slapped him on the shoulder. "Thanks, man."

Dev nodded. Then he tilted his head to the side as he studied Chance. "Lies can fucking destroy, man. Take it from me…with my screwed up past, I know full well the damage they can do."

"I'm not going to mislead Gwen." Not anymore. His gut was knotted now — he needed to see Gwen.

"Good." Dev's voice hardened. "Because I like her. And I like you. So I'd hate to have to kick your ass, but if you make that woman cry again, I just might do it. I hate the sight of a

woman's tears. Nothing worse in the world."
Then he turned away, whistled, and headed for
the leather chairs near the crackling fire place.

***

"Seriously...*what in the hell* were you
thinking?" Sophie Sarantos demanded as she
marched into the interrogation room. Her cheeks
were flushed, her eyes shooting sparks, and her
high heels tapped frantically on the floor. "I'm
your lawyer. I told you to be quiet, I told you—"

"I didn't talk to the cops," Ethan said wearily.
The handcuff was still around his wrist and
annoying the shit out of him. "I talked to Gwen."

Sophie sat down her leather bag. "Gwen?"
Her eyes slammed shut. "Not Gwen
Hawthorne...not the woman you're accused of
stalking."

"Right. That woman. I *told* you that I needed
to see Gwen." He'd asked Sophie again and again
to get him access to Gwen. "She had to know that
I wasn't the one trying to hurt her! She needed to
know—"

"You had secret cameras placed in her
house!" Sophie's eyes flew open. Then her stare
flooded with horror and she glanced toward the
one-way mirror. "Doesn't matter, they can't use
anything I say." Her shoulders straightened.
Sophie was a petite woman, barely skirting five

feet two inches, and she normally wore three inch heels to give herself extra height. "What matters is what *you* say. That's why, for the love of God, just keep your mouth shut." Her heels clicked against the floor. "I am busting ass and pulling every string I have so that you don't spend tonight in general lock-up."

His laughter was rough. "Like I can't handle that. Soph, you…of all people…know what it was like growing up." Because Sophie Sarantos wasn't just his lawyer. She was his friend. They'd been friends since they were kids. Growing up in the wrong part of town, desperately fighting to survive.

Sophie's hands flattened on the table and she leaned forward. Her voice dropped as she said, "I owe you. More than I'll ever be able to repay."

Ethan shook his head.

"You paid for my college. For law school. You—"

"You're one of the few friends I actually have, Sophie. One of the only ones who didn't believe I'd hurt Jena." And she was the one who'd helped him to get Marjorie out of the country. "You've repaid me a million times over."

And that money he'd used to fund her education? Those days…it hadn't come from any respectable business dealings. He'd skirted the law when he was younger, and, sometimes, it was hard to shake his past, no matter how hard he tried.

"I am your friend," she whispered back to him. "So let me do my job and let me help you, okay? No more conversations with Gwen Hawthorne. No more talking with the cops or anyone…just me. This is a serious mess, Ethan. Whoever is stalking Gwen, hell, he's made a life out of ruining you."

Ruining my chance at happiness. He frowned. "The thing is…I never had a chance with her. I knew it, deep down. Knew she was hung up on Chance Valentine."

Sympathy flashed across Sophie's face. "Ethan…"

"I have to figure out who's doing this. You were there back then, Soph, you knew Jena. Were there lovers before me? Anyone who wouldn't let her go?"

She sighed. "She was always so hooked up on you…until the end. I can still remember how upset she was after that last fight with you…when she swore you were cheating on her. That you'd been seen with another woman."

"I never cheated on her." He shook his head. "That wasn't fucking me."

But…maybe someone had wanted Jena to think he'd betrayed her. The same person who'd killed Jena?

Sophie picked up her bag once more. "Try to keep it together, okay? I've got my firm's investigator looking for clues, for any evidence that we can use. Just stay calm until I come back."

Easier said than fucking done.

The door closed behind her. He turned his head. Stared into the mirror. Saw his pale face, his wild eyes.

Calm wasn't exactly a concept for him right then. He stood, as far as the handcuff would let him…and he drove his left fist into that mirror.

The door immediately flew open. Sophie stared at him with horrified eyes. "That's not staying calm!" Then she rushed forward. "Shit, you're bleeding." Her voice rose as she yelled, "We need some help in here!"

But he just stared into the fractured mirror. Stared at himself…

He wasn't the monster, no matter what Gwen thought.

***

Chance stood in front of room 1608. He lifted his hand and knocked. He knew that Gwen would be able to see him through the peephole and she—

"Go away, Chance!" He heard her yell through the door.

Right. She'd definitely seen him. He flattened his hand against the door. "Please, Gwen, we need to talk."

Silence. Then the distinct sounds of locks being turned. The door slowly opened and Gwen stood there, eyeing him suspiciously. "Did you just say the word 'please' to me?"

His head inclined toward her. "It is in my vocabulary."

"I don't remember hearing it before." Her slight body blocked the doorway. His gaze slid over her and lingered on her red toenails. Her feet were bare—and so damn cute.

"I can say please…" His eyes lifted to her face. "I can also say that I'm sorry."

She didn't budge. "Are you?"

"Sorrier than I can fucking say."

Her eyes glinted. "Maybe you should try."

He'd try anything. "I didn't take the job because of your father. I didn't care about his money. I care about you."

"I don't want lies—"

He touched her. He had to. Chance wrapped his hands around her shoulders. "I'm not lying to you. When Will told me that you might be in danger, all I wanted to do was get close to you. I had been thinking about you, dreaming about you, every single night. And even if Will hadn't come to my office, you can bet…I would have come to you. Because I couldn't stay away any longer." His right hand rose and curled under the delicate line of her jaw. "I missed you."

She wasn't speaking.

Hell, he knew how important this moment was. He couldn't afford a screw up with Gwen. She mattered too much. If she wanted him to beg, he would. Pride didn't matter. She did.

So tell her your secrets. Show her what she means to you.

Gwen stepped back. "Come inside."

Yes!

"I'm not forgiving you. I'm just saying that I don't want to have this conversation in the middle of an open doorway." She turned, giving him her back. "Especially if I've got some psycho on my tail—and it sure looks that way. So come in, lock the door, and say whatever it is that you need to say." She paced toward the window. The curtains had been pulled back so the glittering lights of the city shone inside.

He shut the door. Locked it. And tried to find the right words to give her...words that would convince Gwen that *she* truly was the woman he wanted. That her father's money hadn't swayed him.

Never had. Never would.

***

"You've got a rather dangerous client, don't you, Ms. Sarantos?" Lex drawled as he watched the medical team take a cuffed Ethan Barclay down the hallway.

Sophie Sarantos whirled toward him, her hands on her hips. "An accident. My client slipped while in interrogation. Obviously because he was kept too long without food and water and I will make sure the judge hears—"

"Save it, Sophie," Faith said as she followed the med team. "I was staring right through the mirror when your guy stood up and smashed the shit out of it."

Sophie's slightly pointed chin notched into the air and her dark hair—hair nearly a perfect black—slid over her shoulders. "I expect my client to receive the best medical care!" Sophie said as she began to hurry after Faith. "I expect—"

Lex stepped into her path. Her eyes—a shade of blue that shouldn't be legal—narrowed on him. Wow...those blue eyes sure could ice fast. "A moment of your time..." he said. "That's all I need."

"I don't have time to give. My client needs—"

"My name is Lex Jensen, and I work with Chance Valentine."

"Good for you." She started to slide around him.

He just stepped to the left, blocking her path. Lex smiled at her. Unfortunately, he'd been told that he didn't have a particularly nice smile. "Gwen Hawthorne is our client." He figured that was true enough.

"Again, good for you…" She stepped to the right.

So did he.

Her scent—strawberries—rose to tease his nose. He'd always enjoyed the taste of strawberries.

"Get out of my way," Sophie ordered sharply.

"Your client said he was trying to protect Gwen. I'm curious…do you believe that line?"

"It's not my job to believe my clients. My job is to provide them with the best defense possible."

Wrong answer. Well, technically, it was the answer a lawyer was probably supposed to give, but Lex had hoped for more.

From her.

"Guilty or innocent, I guess that doesn't matter," he muttered.

She put her hands on his shoulders. The move totally caught him off-guard—as did the heat that seemed to streak through him at her touch. Then she leaned forward.

Was she going to kiss him? What the hell? Not that he was complaining.

She pushed up, well, as *up* as she could manage in those sexy shoes of hers and tried to peer over his shoulder.

She wasn't tall enough to make that work. Not even close.

He put his hands on her shoulders and — lightly — pushed her right back down. "My sources tell me that you've known Ethan Barclay since the two of you were kids."

"Good sources. Now just get — "

"Are the two of you lovers?"

"What? No!"

"Ever have been?"

Her eyes became slits of absolute fury. "Get your hands off me."

He removed his hands.

"You don't know me, *Mr. Jensen.* You know nothing about me. So don't dare to question me about my personal life. I am not a woman that you want for an enemy."

No, she wasn't, but he also wasn't backing down. "According to Ethan, someone has been stalking *him* for years. Hurting any woman that he really gets close to. But...then I take a step back and I look at things, and you know what I see?"

"Am I supposed to care?"

The woman had some serious fire. He liked it. "I see you...a constant in his life. A woman who has been there, time and again. Even if you aren't lovers, I bet the guy cares about you." *Probably loves you.* Even if that love wasn't sexual. "So if someone out there really wanted to make sure that Ethan's life was a living hell…wouldn't that person go after you, too?"

Her chin notched higher. "Are you trying to scare me? Because I don't scare easily."

"No, I don't imagine that you do…but it is curious, isn't it?" He waited a beat. "Did you know his ex-fiancée? Jena? Did you—"

"Jena Parker was my best friend. And, no I don't believe that Ethan was responsible for her death. They'd fought, yes, but only because she believed he'd cheated on her. He hadn't." Her words were clipped. "And there is *nothing* else I have to say to you…unless…" Now one black eyebrow arched. "Unless you're going to tell me that Gwen Hawthorne is dropping the charges against my client? In that case, I'll talk to you all night long."

He shook his head.

"Then get your ass out of my way."

He backed up a step.

"Good."

"Sophie?" A man's gruff voice called.

Lex looked down the hallway. He saw the redheaded man who'd roughly greeted him and Chance when they went to Wicked. What had the guy's name been? Something like—

"I'm fine, Daniel," Sophie said. "Just dealing with a jerk."

Daniel's eyes narrowed as he stomped toward Lex. "He's one of those pricks who set up Ethan. Knew he was trouble the minute I saw him at Wicked."

"And it's a good thing you called me then," she said, sending a hot glare Lex's way. "Because we have to make sure that Ethan isn't punished for something he didn't do."

Lex laughed lightly, and he knew the sound was mocking. "Oh, I'm sure there's plenty that guy needs to be punished for."

Her stare was definitely arctic. "You know nothing about him." Then, softer, she added, "Or me."

I'd like to know plenty about you.

But she was already striding past him. She leaned in close and started whispering to Daniel. Lex knew the guy was Ethan's flunky. And the way the fellow was leaning in close to Sophie, well, it looked as if he took orders from her, too.

She must be Ethan's right hand.

So why hasn't she ever been targeted?

She and Daniel slipped down the hallway. The tap of her high heels echoed. Lex watched her walk away, his mind spinning with possibilities. A woman who looked like her, a woman who had constant, intimate access to

Ethan Barclay...the stalker *should* have gone after her.

But he hadn't.

Why?

Suspicion began to churn in his gut. Chance believed they were looking for a man, because a guy in a ski mask had been the one seen at Gwen's apartment the first night. But...that guy had run *to* a van. *To* a van that someone else had been driving. The guy in the ski mask had leapt into the back of the vehicle while the driver raced away from the scene.

Maybe the bastard in the ski mask was just the hired help.

Maybe the real stalker was the one who'd been sitting, all nice and safe, in that driver's seat.

And maybe we're not looking for a man after all. The attacks are all on women. Women who Ethan gets involved with. Maybe the stalker isn't a man trying to hurt him...maybe it's a jealous woman.

Taking his time, he followed Sophie down the hallway.

I'm not the kind of woman that you want for an enemy.

Lex found himself very curious about just what sort of woman she was.

The kind who would kill her best friend, if that friend was with the man Sophie wanted?

He was going to find out.

***

Gwen held her breath as she waited for Chance to speak. She probably should have slammed the door in his face, but when it came to Chance, she was weak.

No...she was just in love.

That had been her problem all along. She'd fallen for the guy. The lust, the physical desire had hit instantly. And the love had come later. Slowly, easily, and she hadn't even realized that she was in trouble until it was too late.

Then she'd looked up at him on Christmas Eve. Seen him standing there, all alone, and she'd just wanted to be with him.

"I didn't have much growing up," Chance said.

What? She shook her head. Why was he —

"Actually, I didn't have anything. My family grew up on a farm in Georgia, a farm that went broke when I was ten years old. My father drank himself to death after that and my mom...she didn't live much longer after he passed."

Gwen took a step toward him. "Chance, I-I'm sorry." Because she could feel his pain and she'd always hated for Chance to be in any sort of pain.

"Cancer," he murmured. And his gaze had turned distant, as if he were seeing the past. "She'd had some warning signs, but...hell, she and my dad were so focused on saving the farm, so she just kept putting off her doctor visits. No money, no time…and then when she finally went in…" His lips twisted into a sad smile. "There really was no time left by then. She lived for six months. I told her good-bye when I was sixteen."

She'd walked across the room. Gwen didn't remember that. Hadn't she just taken one step a moment before? She was almost touching him now and Gwen wanted—so badly—to wrap her arms around Chance and take away his pain.

"I didn't have any other family, so I wound up in foster care. That's where I met Dev and Lex. Dev had big dreams, even back then. The guy could do anything with a computer. He got a scholarship, got the hell out of the system. Lex and I…we joined the military. Turned out I was pretty good at fighting."

She wet her lips. "You're pretty good at a lot of things."

He glanced down at the floor, then back up at her. "I'm not good…with you."

What was that supposed to mean?

Chance rubbed his hand over his jaw, and his palm rasped against the dark stubble there. "I never say the right words with you. I never feel like I do the right things. You and your father— you live in a mansion and I—"

"That's my father's house. I live in a two bedroom apartment." She kept her hands by her side. Tricky hands. They were still itching to reach out to him. "And do you seriously think I care about how much money you have?"

"I'm good now." His shoulders straightened with what she knew was pride. "I worked hard. I saved. And I'll always have enough for whatever I need now. For whatever you need."

"Uh, yeah, okay, I can take care of my own things—"

"I'm saying the wrong shit again." He huffed out a hard breath. "I meant...I don't need your father's money. I didn't agree to act as your bodyguard because of what he was paying me or what he offered to do for me. I have plenty of my own money now. Plenty of contacts. I don't need him."

"Then why did you take the case? Why lie to me? Why not just tell me the truth?"

"I took the case...because I wanted to be close to you. I wanted to make sure you were safe." He closed the last bit of distance between them. His hand lifted and skimmed lightly across her jaw. That one touch—so simple—sent heat coursing through her. "I lied...because I was scared. I was afraid that if I told you the truth, hell, I don't know, that you'd send me away. That you wouldn't want me near you because you didn't feel the same way that I do."

Her heart was about to jump right out of her chest. "How do you feel?"

"I feel like I was a fucking fool." He bent toward her. "I let you go when you were right in front of me. You were offering me every dream I'd had, but I didn't think I was good enough for you. Didn't think I should even be touching you."

"You're touching me now," she told him, her voice husky.

"I want to give you the world, Gwen. I want to give you—"

"I don't want the world." She rose onto her toes and decided that it was time to take another risk. Maybe she'd get hurt again. Maybe she'd crash and burn, but she'd be brave enough to try. Brave enough to fight for what she wanted. "All I want...I want you."

Her fingers curled behind his neck. Chance pressed his mouth to hers. The kiss wasn't wild and frantic. It was soft. Careful. As if he were afraid of scaring her off.

He should know...she wasn't going to be afraid. Not of him.

So she slipped her tongue over the crease of his lips.

"Gwen..."

"Don't be careful with me. You're the one I want. Show me that you want me, too." He'd said that he had trouble telling her how he felt. Fine. Gwen wanted Chance to show her instead.

When he kissed her again, his lips were parted. Better...Gwen's teeth closed lightly over his bottom lip and she bit, tugging.

He growled and his hold tightened on her. *Much* better.

"No more lies," she ordered softly. "Not from you. Not from me. Give me everything you have..." Her tongue licked across his lower lip. "And I'll give you all that I have, too." No holding back.

"Everything," he promised her.

Then he kissed her. Deep. Hard. Wild. Perfect.

***

The bitch wasn't going to walk away. Ethan was in jail, just what the asshole deserved. He should rot in there.

But Gwen Hawthorne...she didn't get to just slip away now. Because if she was still out there, Ethan would think he had a chance. He'd think he could be happy.

He never would be. His life would be just as fucked...

As mine.

CHAPTER TEN

Gwen was in his arms. She was kissing him. Doing that sexy little bite thing on his bottom lip and generally driving him mad with lust.

Chance backed her up against the window. Caged her there with his body. His hands were sliding over her, stripping her as fast as he could. She hadn't told him to go to hell. Hadn't kicked his ass out of her hotel room. She was giving him a second chance, one he probably didn't deserve, but he'd take it.

He'd take everything that Gwen had to give to him.

That had been their deal, their promise...*everything*.

"Don't be gentle," Gwen said. "I like it rough. I like you...hard."

His cock was so full it was about to burst right out of his jeans. He caught hold of her shirt and his rough hands sent buttons flying. "Gwen—"

She laughed. The sound of her laughter nearly drove him to his knees.

She was wearing a black bra, one that pushed up her breasts and had him nearly drooling as he stared at her. He touched her breasts, cradling them, and she gasped at the contact.

"More," Gwen said.

He'd give her plenty more.

Chance lifted her into his arms. Gwen gave a little yelp and her arms locked around him. "Chance, wait, what are you doing?"

He kissed her again. She gave that little moan in the back of her throat—the one that made his cock twitch. "Remember…before I told you….I'd have you in a big-ass bed."

And such a perfect bed was steps away. He wouldn't screw her against the wall or a window. He'd make love with her, for the rest of the night. In that bed.

He lowered Gwen to her feet. Stripped her. Stroked her as he slid those clothes away from her smooth skin. Then Chance pushed her back on the bed. His hands trailed up her legs. Up, up. She was bare and wet and warm. So perfect. His fingers dipped between her thighs.

Gwen reached for him.

"No."

She froze. Their gazes held.

"I get to make you scream first." He had plenty of dreams to live out. "Put your hands over your head, baby. Lock your fingers around the pillow. Tighten your muscles and try to hold still for me." Because that stillness…that tightness of her muscles…it would lead to such pleasure.

Gwen's hands lifted.

"Remember," he whispered. "Stay still…" He slid between her legs. Pushed them farther apart. He was still dressed because the clothes helped to give him a little more control. If he were naked, he'd be in her.

Not yet. Make her scream first. Make her come. Make her forget any other lover.

Because he'd forgotten all of his past lovers. Only Gwen mattered.

He put his mouth on her. Gwen immediately jerked and her hands flew down. Her fingers wrapped around his shoulders.

He stilled. So hard to do, especially when he just wanted to taste her. "No, baby, not yet…put your hands back up…"

Her nails sank into his skin.

He blew lightly over her exposed sex.

"Chance…"

"Back up," he ordered.

Her hands rose.

"Good. Now arch up to me…open to me…"

He put his mouth back on her. He licked her, he stroked, and he pretty much went out of his mind and when he felt her body shaking, when she was quivering and when—

"Chance!"

Yes! He surged up. Yanked for the condom he'd put in his wallet and he was in her within seconds. Driving deep.

Her hands were on him, her arms holding him tightly. She was still climaxing when he plunged balls-deep into her. Still coming around him as he thrust, again and again, and her release kept going—he could feel her pleasure and it propelled him right into his own climax.

A climax that seemed to completely consume him. That had him choking out her name and holding her tight.

That had him realizing...*I never want to let her go.*

***

Gwen's eyes opened. The hotel room was dark...the only light came from outside, spilling in through the curtains that she'd left open. She was naked in that big bed, and the sheets were soft against her body.

Naked, but not alone.

Gwen turned her head. Chance was there, asleep next to her. His arm was wrapped around her stomach, and she found that oddly sweet. He was still holding her, even while he slept.

He was naked, too. They'd made love again—at least twice more during the night. The pleasure had washed over her, so hard and strong. Taking away fear and anger, leaving her with hope. Hope for her future—a future with Chance.

Gwen eased toward him. A month ago, she wouldn't have thought that a future with Chance would be possible. A week ago…same thing.

But right then…

Gwen leaned close. She pressed a kiss to Chance's throat. Softly, because she didn't want to wake—

His eyes opened. His arms locked around her and he rolled Gwen beneath him. "Missed you…" His voice was gruff, little more than a growl. "Shouldn't have let you go…now only have dreams…" He was holding her so tightly. "Have to find you again…can't let go…"

"Chance, I'm here." *He thinks this is a dream.* "It's me."

Silence.

She felt his awareness then, in the stiffness of his muscles and saw it in the way his head whipped up. In the darkness, his eyes gleamed down at her.

"Had so many dreams…" Chance said. "All about you. Then I'd wake up, and you'd be gone."

His words tore at her heart. And to think…Chance had said that he couldn't say the right things to her. "I'm not gone." *I'm not going anyplace.*

She was exactly where she wanted to be...well, actually...

Gwen pushed against his shoulders. Chance immediately rolled back. "Gwen, baby, I—"

She climbed on top of him. "You weren't the only one with dreams. I think I told you that before." She straddled him. Her sex brushed over his cock. His already swelling cock. The guy certainly had stamina. Her fingers slid over his chest. "I want to live out one of my dreams right now, too."

His fingers closed around her hips. "Gwen?"

She rubbed her sex over his cock. Skin on skin. Nothing between them. She kept up that friction, rubbing lightly, and Gwen could feel herself getting wet for him. "I'm on the pill."

His hold tightened, nearly bruising. "I'm clean."

She wanted to be with him like this, with nothing between them. "So am I." She wrapped her fingers around his wrists and pushed them back near his head, chaining them against the pillow. "So now it's your turn, Chance. Let's see just how long you can stay still."

Her left hand slid down and she pushed the head of his cock against the opening of her sex. She arched and took him in, not too deep, not yet. His free hand immediately tried to grab for her hip.

Her left hand caught his wrist again, and she forced his hand back up to the pillow. "That didn't last long." Her voice was husky, her body aching. "Let's try again." And she took all of him inside in one long, hot drive.

She moaned. He growled. It was perfect.

She slid up, then down again, keeping her pace slow. Gwen's nipples were tight, sensitive peaks, and the long length of his erection slid over her, *into her*, at just the right angle.

Gwen stared into Chance's eyes. She saw them go darker, saw the desire flaring. But he wasn't moving his hands from that pillow, wasn't touching her.

Good. To reward him, Gwen's motions became faster. Harder. Her breath panted out and she used her hold on his wrists to better brace her body. Her heart thundered in her chest, her knees dug into that mattress, and his cock was so big as it pushed deeper into her. Again and again and again...

"*Can't stay still...*" His voice rasped at her. "Can't...control is..."

She stared into his eyes. Saw it happen.

Control is gone.

He lunged up, wrapped his arms around her and Gwen laughed with the surge of power that she felt. She wanted him this way. So wild for her that nothing else mattered. She wanted to know that she could make him this way. It was only fair really...

Because he drove her way over the edge of her own control.

They wrecked the bed. Rolling, twisting, nearly fighting for the pleasure. The release hit Gwen first, a pounding, body-shaking orgasm that had her crying out for him, and then Chance was with her. The hot surge of his release filled her as he held her so tightly. The pleasure didn't crest—it kept going and going and she almost couldn't catch her breath.

He kissed her. Savored her. And her sex greedily clamped around him.

"I always knew..." Gwen whispered. "It would be like this...with us."

Chance kissed her again. "So did I." He pulled her against him. Curled his body around hers and made sure the covers were tucked around Gwen.

She smiled as her eyes began to close. She was safe. She was happy. She was—

"It's what I was afraid of..."

Gwen almost didn't hear his whisper. Almost.

"That I'd have you," he said softly. "And never be able to let you go."

***

The ringing of his phone woke Chance hours later. His eyes opened. He squinted as he tried to adjust. Bright light poured in from the window, momentarily blinding him.

The phone kept ringing.

"Want me to get it?" Gwen's sleep voice murmured.

And Gwen was there. Cuddled against him. So fucking perfect and very much not a dream. Her tousled hair slid over his pillow and her eyes were still closed. She was naked and her arm was around him.

She's real.

He swallowed. "I...got it." He reached over her. Grabbed the phone. Saw Lex's number on the screen and tensed as he put the phone to his ear. "Lex, what is it?" he demanded as the last bit of sleepiness vanished.

"Ethan's out," Lex said flatly. "The judge granted bail first thing this morning."

Chance sat up. The news wasn't completely unexpected. It wasn't welcome, but it wasn't unexpected.

"He's with his lawyer now. And...there's something else you need to know about Sophie Sarantos. I've been doing some checking on her."

"Sophie? Why?" He knew Sophie Sarantos. In D.C., most people wound up at the same parties, at some point. Sophie was smart, driven, and he'd heard that she was on track to becoming one of the highest paid defense lawyers in the area.

"Because from what I can tell, Sophie is the one constant in the guy's life. They might not be lovers, but they're close. If some psycho out there really is attacking all the women Ethan cares about, then why didn't he go after her? She's the one in the limelight with him most times. The one photographed at his side. She seems like the obvious choice of a target."

Gwen had sat up, too. She pulled the covers with her. She was leaning in close and Chance knew she was listening to Lex's words.

"I found out that Sophie's parents died when she was seventeen. A gunman broke into their house and killed them both. That shooter was never identified, the murder never solved. But...medical records Dev managed to access indicated that there was a...history there."

Managed to access? Right. He knew Dev had probably hacked into the system.

"Sophie had over a dozen broken bones during her teenage years. She was admitted to the hospital again and again, and though the docs suspected abuse, no charges were ever filed against her parents. The police cleared them every time."

Chance met Gwen's worried gaze.

"There was absolutely no evidence left at the scene of her parents' murder. Nothing at all.

But…but my gut is telling me there is a lot more going on here. Sophie's past is bloody and dark and with her tied so closely to Ethan — *she should have been the stalker's victim*."

"But she isn't," Chance said softly, "Gwen is."

Gwen's gaze never faltered.

Chance understood exactly what Lex was saying. "You think she could be our perp."

"I think the stalker *should* have gone after her," Lex responded carefully, "but he didn't…and I want to know why."

"So do I." Maybe he and Gwen needed to have a little sit down with the lawyer. "Keep me posted."

"And you keep your lady safe," Lex said.

"Count on it."

***

"You're welcome," Sophie told Ethan as the driver shut the back door of Ethan's car, sealing them inside. "Because, yes, I did manage to work a minor miracle in there…"

"I'm out on a million dollar bond," Ethan said as he leaned his head back against the seat and closed his eyes. "That's not so much a miracle as it is huge chunk of change." He heard the driver's door shut and the vehicle began to accelerate.

Sophie didn't speak.

Hell. His eyes opened. "Thank you, Soph," he told her. "You know I can't repay the shit you do for me. I'd be lost without you."

"So you say." Her smile was bittersweet. "But I'm the one who'd be alone. After my parents…you were all I had."

Her parents. His gut clenched when he remembered that particular nightmare. He'd wanted to kill Sophie's father for years, and…in a blink, Sophie's hell had been over. He knew her secrets, just as she knew his. Secrets that he would take to the grave.

His fingers reached for hers. Twined. They'd never been lovers. They never would be. They were family. Closer than blood.

He glanced toward the front of the car. His driver and sometimes bodyguard, Daniel, had just braked at the light. "Take Sophie home first. I want to make sure she's safe."

Sophie laughed. "Right. Because I don't know how to take care of myself. Have you forgotten that most of the criminals in this city know me on a first name basis?"

His hold on her tightened. "You matter to me. I want you safe."

Her eyelids lowered. She stared down at their hands. "He's targeted women close to you."

Yes, the bastard had.

"Lex Jensen made me wonder…" Sophie stopped talking and glanced out of her window.

"Soph?"

"He works with Chance. He, um, stopped me at the station."

Ethan waited, wondering where this was going.

"I was never targeted."

"That's a fucking good thing." He brought her hand to his lips. Pressed a quick kiss to her knuckles. "Because without you, I'd go insane."

She glanced back at him, a faint smile curving her lips. "How do you think I'd be without you? You've been my rock for all of these years."

"I'll always be here for you."

Sophie nodded. Her dark hair was pulled back and her eyes — they seemed even bigger without the thick tumble of her hair falling near her heart-shaped face. Bigger, but…sad?

"It's going to be all right," Ethan told her. How many times had he said those words or something similar to Sophie over the years? "We're going to find him. We're going to stop him."

"You've said that before."

Unfortunately, he had.

Exhaling slowly, he looked toward the front of the vehicle. Daniel turned the car to the left, not saying a word to them, and they headed for Sophie's home.

CHAPTER ELEVEN

The elevator doors opened and Gwen stepped out into the lush hotel lobby. Plenty of people were buzzing in that space — guests checking out, bell hops carrying luggage.

And Dev was there, standing in the middle of the lobby, staring right at her and Chance. Dev's face appeared grim. Dark circles were under his eyes and a serious five o'clock shadow lined his jaw.

"We've got a problem," he said as they approached him.

Another one? Gwen was really over any new problems. She had more than enough to deal with as it was —

"Marjorie West is dead."

Gwen stilled.

"Ethan gave her a new identity and sent her to Europe, yeah, that part of his little story was true, but the woman sure as hell didn't get away scot free." Dev rolled back his shoulders. "I kept digging until I found out what became of her. It took a while and some serious string pulling…but an unknown female was killed by a hit and run driver in Paris, four months after Marjorie supposedly started her new life."

"You don't know that it was her," Gwen said. "You can't know, you can't—"

"I compared that victim's dental records with Marjorie's. They were a match."

She could only stare blankly at him.

"You don't want to know the connections he has," Chance said, his voice rough. "Or the laws that he probably broke to make that match."

Dev cleared his throat. "Laws were bent, not broken. There's a difference." Then he shook his head. "Based on the police reports for that accident…"

She was too numb to be surprised that he'd accessed French police records.

"The hit and run scene went down much like the recent one with Gwen here. The driver was waiting on the side of the street, waiting for his moment to strike. Witnesses said he didn't slow down, that he deliberately accelerated when he aimed for his prey. He swerved to hit her, and when she went down, he roared away."

He. "So it is a man. It's not Sophie." Gwen had spoken to Sophie Sarantos at dozens of charity functions over the years. She'd…liked the other woman. Sure, Sophie could be a little withdrawn, but she was nice. Dedicated. She cared about helping victims of domestic abuse, and Gwen had worked with her on a special domestic violence prevention fundraiser at the gallery just last spring. They'd raised over fifty thousand dollars at that event, and Sophie had been crying at the end of the night. Silent tears that she'd swiped away before she thought anyone saw them.

I saw them.

When she'd overheard Lex talking about Sophie, Gwen's first instinct had been denial because well...

Sophie seems too nice.

But she knew appearances could be deceiving.

"Actually..." Dev winced. "I don't know the driver's sex. The windows were tinted, so no one got a good look at the driver. The perp could have been a man...or a woman. But what I do know is this...whoever we're looking for, the perp doesn't let his prey get away from him. If he tracked Marjorie all the way across the Atlantic Ocean, that should sure as hell tell us something. He doesn't give up. He doesn't stop."

Not until his prey is dead.

"That does tell us something." Chance took Gwen's hand. "Ethan said that only he and Sophie knew where Marjorie had gone. If it was just the two of them—and Marjorie wound up dead—then one of them killed her."

Sophie or Ethan.

"Lex needs to move in on Sophie," Chance said. "And I'm going to have another little chat with Ethan. One that doesn't involve the cops."

Gwen shook her head. "No, that isn't a good plan. You can't—"

He turned toward her. "He was choosing every word he said in that police station. He knew the cops were watching. Knew that every word he said was being monitored. The guy wasn't going to screw up there."

"Chance—"

He kissed her. A quick, hot, open-mouthed kiss. "I'd do anything for you." His words were low and she was aware of Dev easing back a step. "I'd fight for you, lie, hell, I'd kill without a second's hesitation."

She grabbed his arms. Held tight. "I don't want you killing for me."

"You're what matters to me." He searched her eyes. "I need you to know that. I fucked up before, but I won't ever do it again. I...I love you, Gwen."

No, no, he had not just said—

"I want to end this nightmare. I don't want a threat hanging over you. I don't want you looking over your shoulder every time you go out."

Gwen couldn't look away from him.

"I want you safe. I need you to be safe. And when this is all over..." He drew in a ragged breath. "If you…if you want, we could go forward. See if we can make it together. Because I want to be with you."

From the corner of her eye, she saw Dev take another step back.

"Maybe I've screwed up too much," Chance muttered, "and—"

Now she was the one to stand on her toes. To brush her lips against his. "We are going forward." Nothing would stop them. Because he wasn't the only one who'd fight…she'd fight for him. Lie. Kill. Did he think he was the only one who'd be pushed to the edge—and beyond?

He smiled at her. When he smiled, the man was absolutely gorgeous.

I love him.

"No more fear," Gwen said. *Sophie or Ethan.* "Let's see where this ends." Ended…for the stalker.

But for her and Chance—*things will begin.*

Chance pulled out his phone. Got Lex on the line. She heard him updating the other man, telling him to close in on Sophie.

Then Chance put the phone down. He stared into Gwen's eyes. "This isn't going to be easy. To get the truth, I'll have to play dirty."

So will I. She wasn't going to flinch away from what was coming. Two women were dead, and Gwen wouldn't be next.

She had far too much to live for.

***

Lex stared up the brownstone. Sophie's home. She'd gone in an hour before, right after Ethan had dropped her off. Lex had watched as Ethan walked Sophie to the door, as he'd pressed a light kiss to her cheek.

Then he'd left her. Sophie had been inside since then. Plenty of cars had gone up and down the street, but Sophie hadn't stirred again.

He crossed the street. More snow had fallen during the night, and when he reached the sidewalk, the snow crunched lightly beneath his feet. He climbed the steps leading to her place. The cold air chilled his lungs. Lex pressed the doorbell...and waited.

Nothing.

He pressed his finger against the doorbell again. Still no response.

Leaning back, he peered through the window on the right. All of the lights were out in her house. Everything seemed so quiet. Empty.

But...he'd seen Sophie go inside. She had to still be there.

Unless she slipped away. Unless she slipped right by me and I didn't even realize it.

But—

Hell, no. He was too good for that.

Wasn't he?

Lex pounded on the door. "Sophie! Sophie, open up! It's Lex Jensen. I need to talk to you!"

***

Chance parked in front of Wicked. The club looked shut down. They'd already stopped by Ethan's home, but the door man there had sworn that Ethan wasn't in the building.

Since Ethan's home-away-from-home was Wicked, Chance had headed there.

A car was parked out front and when Chance walked by it, he pressed his hand to the hood. Still warm.

Chance strode to the main door. Gwen was at his side. He grabbed for the handle. Locked. So Chance pounded on the door. No answer.

But the car is still warm...so I know he's inside.

"I'll go around back," Dev said, inclining his head. "That way, we can make sure we've got both doors covered."

Chance nodded. They would be getting inside to Ethan. One way or another.

Dev hurried away.

Chance looked over at Gwen. She had her phone out. "Who are you —"

The front door opened. He recognized the man standing there. It was the redheaded guy he'd met the first time he and Gwen had come to Wicked for the fucked-up, sit-down with Ethan.

The man glanced nervously over his shoulder, then looked at Gwen. "You need to leave," he said.

Chance stepped in front of Gwen. "We need to see Ethan."

"Daniel, please," Gwen said. "We have to get in there. This has to end."

Daniel licked his lips. "It's not safe. I-I heard him talking. He...he's not right." He eased toward them. "Take her and go."

Chance's body tensed. "What did you hear?"

"I was driving him...and Sophie. He was so careful with Sophie, but..." Again, he inched closer to them. The guy's hands were shaking. "After he left her, he lost it." His voice was a low whisper. "He came back here, and he's been wrecking the place."

Chance heard a crash from inside the building.

Gwen gasped.

"He's dangerous..." Daniel's eyes were wide. "I think...I think he wants to kill Gwen. You have to get her out of here."

***

Sophie wasn't answering her door. No sound at all was coming from inside her place. That shit couldn't be good.

Lex hurried down the steps and stalked around the side of the brownstone. He hadn't gone far when he saw the footprints. The tracks were so clear in the snow—leading to the window, then leading away. More snow was expected to hit at any time, so soon those footprints would be covered, but for the moment...

Someone went into Sophie's house.

He rushed to that window, leaving his own trail in the snow. The footprints he passed were big—heavy treads left from boots. The latch on the window was broken, and Lex shoved it up. "Sophie!" As soon as he opened that window, the scent of gas hit him. Bitter, like rotten eggs. "Fuck, Sophie!' He leapt through that window and rushed into the house. A chair was overturned in her den. A lamp smashed. And Sophie was there, crumpled on the floor like a broken doll. The shattered lamp was near her shoulder and blood from a deep gash on her head had dripped onto the carpet.

"Sophie!" He checked for her pulse. Weak, but still there. "I'm getting you out of here. You're going to be okay." He hoped.

Lex lifted her into his arms, held her carefully, and moved as fast as he could for the door. That smell was overwhelming now, and he knew that whoever had knocked her out...the bastard had deliberately left a gas leak at her house.

She could have asphyxiated in there. Or maybe the killer had planned to leave her in the house for a while, trapped, helpless, and then…he could have come back and with the flick of a match—

Boom.

He rushed through the front door and took her out of that house. Lex didn't want to take any chances—if that brownstone blew, they needed to be far away from it. He rushed across the street, with Sophie still in his arms. She started to stir when they reached the other side. Her eyelashes flickered, then lifted.

"E-Ethan…?"

"It's Lex." He wanted to beat the hell out of Ethan. "It's all right. Ethan isn't going to hurt you again. I won't let him." She was so delicate. Felt so fragile in his arms.

Sophie began to struggle in his arms. Tremors shook her and she said, "E-Ethan…Ethan…E-Ethan…" She was chanting his name again and again, and Lex lowered her to the ground. He wrapped his arms around her, holding her as tightly as he could, and he called nine-one-one. When the dispatcher came on the line, he told her to get an ambulance and cops to Sophie's address, as fast as they damn well could. And he asked for Detective Faith Chestang.

Because she needed to know what was happening.

The next call he made was to Chance. Still holding tightly to Sophie, he had the phone at his ear. Sophie was whispering Ethan's name as the phone rang. Once. Twice —

***

When his phone rang, Chance yanked it out of his pocket and glanced at the screen. Lex. He answered immediately even as he turned to face Gwen. "Lex, look, we've got a problem with Ethan—"

"He just tried to kill Sophie!" Lex's voice snarled. "I had to carry her out of her home. He knocked her out, turned on her gas...shit, she's bad."

Gwen's eyes were full of worry as she stared at Chance.

"All she'll say," Lex continued grimly, "is the bastard's name. Over and over and—"

The worry in Gwen's gaze gave way to stark terror. Only she wasn't staring straight at Chance. She was looking over his shoulder.

"Chance, behind you!" Gwen screamed. She shoved against him, trying to knock him out of the way.

And that was when the gunshot rang out.

CHAPTER TWELVE

Gwen tried to push Chance out of the way, but he twisted his body, protecting her — *damn him!* — and the bullet slammed into him.

Chance didn't go down, though. "Run," he told Gwen and he pushed her away. "Go!"

He spun toward the attacker — Daniel — and she saw Chance pulling out his own weapon. He'd grabbed it from his vehicle when they'd first approached Wicked, but he'd holstered the weapon beneath his jacket. Now it was taking too long for him to get that weapon out and —

Daniel fired again. The bullet drove into Chance's stomach.

"No!" Gwen screamed. She lunged forward when Chance slumped to the ground. She grabbed for him and his blood covered her hands. "Chance, no!"

"Move away from him." Daniel's voice was too high, cracking with…excitement?

Gwen put her hand over Chance's wound. The gun had fallen from his hand when he'd slumped down. His eyes were closed but…

He's alive.

"I'm not moving," Gwen said. Dev was close by. He would've heard the shot. He'd be coming to help them any moment.

"Then I'll shoot you right here."

She glared up at Daniel. He had his gun aimed right at her head.

"And after you're dead, I'll put a bullet in Chance Valentine's heart. He might be able to survive the injuries he has so far…but a bullet to the heart?" He laughed. "Dead fucking man."

Gwen pressed down harder, trying to stop that blood flow.

"Come inside with me, and I'll leave him. Give him a fifty-fifty shot of survival." Daniel's lips twisted in a cold grin. "I never cared about him. He doesn't matter. You matter. Ethan matters."

Her body was numb with cold.

"Move now, or I will kill him."

Her fingers slid away from Chance. *I love you.* He knew that, didn't he? He had to know, he had to—

Chance's eyes opened. "Gwen, *no.*" He reached for her.

But Daniel yanked Gwen to her feet. He locked one arm around her neck and put the gun to her head.

Chance struggled to rise. To reach for the gun that had slipped from his fingers.

Daniel kicked the weapon out of Chance's reach.

"You know…" Daniel's voice actually sounded as if he were considering the situation. "I think she loved you, Valentine. Enough to die for you. Lucky sonofabitch." Then he hauled Gwen back, pulling her inside of Wicked.

Chance tried to crawl after them. "Gwen!"

"I love you," she whispered. Daniel's hold was too strong. She was clawing at his arm, but she couldn't break free.

He dragged her across the threshold then slammed the door shut and locked them inside Wicked.

"Ethan's waiting for you," he said, his breath blowing against her ear. "Come on…this has been such a long fucking time coming." He was hauling her across the floor.

She kicked back at him, trying to do as much damage to him as she could. Chance was safe—for the moment. Now she had to survive. She had to stop Daniel. She had to—

They were now in front of the bar in Wicked. Ethan was there. Tied to a chair. Thick ropes were around his chest, his arms, and his legs. A gag had been shoved over his mouth and tied in place. Ethan's head sagged forward, but she could see the blood sliding down his cheeks. He appeared to have been slashed across the face—

one deep slash slid across his left cheek and one streaked across his right.

Blood also soaked his shirt. *Stabbed.* From the look of things, he'd been stabbed again and again...

A table had overturned next to him, and she remembered the crash she'd heard when she and Chance had been outside Wicked, when Daniel had been feeding them that line of bull about Ethan wrecking the place in a fury. Now she realized that Ethan must have managed to push over that table. He'd probably been trying to alert them, to get help—

It's too late for help now.

A low whimper slipped from her because of the obvious abuse Ethan had endured.

"Not so handsome anymore, is he?" Daniel asked. "Not the fucking perfect son anymore."

Ethan's head tipped back. He stared at Gwen with dawning horror in his eyes. He twisted in his bonds.

"Before I kill you..." Now Gwen realized that Daniel was speaking to Ethan, not her. "I thought you'd like to see Gwen once more. You know...to tell her good-bye."

Ethan's eyes were frantic.

"After that, I'm going to kill her." Daniel laughed. A truly chilling sound. "I'll kill her, then you...*big brother.*"

Gwen shook her head. Had he just said…*brother?*

***

Chance grabbed the gun. His fingers were soaked with blood so the gun nearly slipped away, but he just tightened his hold on it. He rose slowly, fighting the pain and the nausea that rolled through him. One bullet was in his back. One in his gut.

The bastard should have killed him. Because only death would have stopped Chance.

I'm coming for you, Gwen. One step. Two. He pushed the pain back. Focused on her. He reached out for the door.

Locked.

Like that would slow him down.

He pointed that gun and fired. The lock didn't give so he fired again. If he had to, he'd claw down that door because he *was* getting inside. Chance was getting to Gwen.

I love you.

He'd heard those words from her. Seen the love in her eyes. Chance would kill the fool who'd threatened her. *Kill him.*

The lock gave way and Chance shoved open the door.

***

At the thunder of gunfire, Daniel spun around. "What in the hell?" His hold eased on Gwen as he surged toward the dying blast.

That moment of confusion was just what Gwen needed. She tore free of him and raced toward the nearest chair.

"No!" Daniel lunged after her. "Stop!"

Gwen threw a chair at him even as he fired. She felt the burn of the bullet graze over her arm. She grabbed for another chair. She lifted it —

His gun was aimed at her again. Pointing at her heart.

"Devlin is coming," she said, her words rushing out quickly as she kept that chair up, her only weapon. "He was out back. He's the one who—"

Daniel laughed. "The dark-haired one? Yeah, I already took him out."

Gwen shook her head.

"I used my knife on him, so you wouldn't hear the attack. Did it nice and fast. I left him in a pool of blood..."

Ethan muttered frantically behind his gag.

Daniel's gaze flew toward him. "What? It's your fault. It's all your fault. You're the one dear old Dad chose. He lived with you and your bitch of a mother, but you weren't grateful. He turned his back on me and my mom, but you still hated him. You still—"

Gunfire. Thundering. Erupting. Slamming into Daniel and he jerked like a marionette on a string. He tried to turn toward the shooter, but Gwen slammed her chair into him. Daniel fell, and his gun slid across the floor. Gwen scrambled after it. She grabbed the weapon, fumbled, aimed it, and saw...

Chance stood just a few feet away. Bloody. Swaying a little. And with his weapon still up and pointed toward Daniel.

Gwen ran to Chance. She locked her arms around him and held on to him as tightly as she could. Tears were filling her eyes and spilling down her cheeks. Chance was alive. Strong. With her. He was—

Falling.

She couldn't stop him. They both crashed to the floor. Frantic, she yelled, "Chance!"

There was so much blood. Too much. She looked behind him and saw that he'd left a trail of blood as he walked into the room.

"Can't...feel legs now..." Chance whispered.

Her heart nearly stopped.

She grabbed his hand.

"Can't...feel you...so cold..."

No. No! "Chance, please, please don't do this. I love you!"

His lips lifted, in just the faintest smile. The smile that had stolen her heart so long ago. "Always...love you...do anything...for you..."

Gwen could hear the scream of sirens. The police were coming. Someone must have reported the shots. Police—and an ambulance? "Help is almost here. We're both going to make it. We'll be okay."

Ethan was muttering, growling behind his gag, but she didn't look at him. She couldn't look away from Chance.

Even though his eyes were closing.

"No!" Gwen yelled. "You say you'll do anything for me? Then don't die! Don't you dare die! You live with me. You live for me!"

His eyelids flickered.

"Please don't leave me," Gwen said. Her hands were pressing to the wound over his stomach. She had to stop the blood flow. Had to help him. Nothing else mattered. Only Chance. Only him. She kept talking to him. Kept applying pressure and the minutes seemed to crawl by. The sirens were louder. Closer. Help had to be nearly there. *Hurry, hurry, hurry—*

"Drop the weapon!"

That was Faith's voice.

Gwen looked up, blinking past her tears. Faith was a few feet away. The detective's gun was in her hand and she was pointing it at Gwen.

I don't have a weapon. I had to put it down so I could help Chance. I had to—

"I will kill you," Faith said, voice fierce.

She isn't talking to me.

Gwen glanced over her shoulder. Daniel was on his knees. He had a knife in his hand, and he'd been heading toward Gwen.

Ethan was still snarling behind his gag.

Uniformed cops raced in behind Faith.

Daniel dropped the knife.

"Good move, asshole," Faith said. The cops closed in on Daniel.

Gwen looked back down at Chance. His eyes were open. On her. "Chance?" *Don't go! Don't!*

"Anything…" he told her, his voice a bare breath of sound. "For you." His fingers slid toward her. "Anything…"

Medics rushed in and they pushed Gwen back. She watched as the team swarmed into action. "Devlin," Gwen said, voice sounding like a stranger's to her own ears. Too cold. Too hollow. But she had to tell Faith about the other man. "He's out back. Daniel said he attacked him. Dev needs help, too!"

Faith motioned with her left hand and cops rushed toward the back of Wicked.

When the medics hoisted Chance on a stretcher, Gwen raced after them. Snow was falling outside. A light covering, reminding her of so many other times.

Reminding her of a kiss with Chance, a kiss hot enough to melt that snow.

"Gwen!" Someone grabbed her arm. No, not just someone. She shook past the fog of memories that had surrounded her and found herself gazing into her father's frantic eyes. He stared at her a moment, almost as if he were afraid to believe she was really there, in front of him, then he yanked her against his chest and held her in a grip that hurt. "I was afraid," he told her, voice gruff, "so afraid I'd get here and you'd be dead. When Faith called me…she was already racing over here and I didn't think either of us would get here in time."

Her tears fell harder. "Dad…it's Chance. He was shot protecting me." She pulled away from him and saw that Chance had already been loaded into the back of the ambulance. "I have to go with him. I can't lose him!"

Her father glanced over at the ambulance. Swore. And then he was running with her to the back of that open vehicle. Gwen tried to jump in the back, but the EMT waved her away. "No, ma'am," he said, "this man is critical. If you aren't family—"

"She is his family!" Her father shouted. "She's the woman he loves and you're letting her back there or your ass will be on the street next week looking for a new job." He puffed out his chest. "Son, you don't know what kind of hell you're—"

Gwen shoved her dad back before he could finish his threat. She jumped into the back of the ambulance just as its siren roared on again. Gwen scooted over so she wouldn't get in the way of the EMTs and then…

"I love you…" Chance's hand reached for her. "My…Gwen."

She wrapped her hand around his. The ambulance lurched forward.

"Won't go…anywhere…" Chance told her, even as his eyes drifted closed, "without you."

"You'd better not," Gwen said. Because she didn't want to imagine the rest of her life, not without him in it.

***

By the time the ambulance rounded the corner, Will Hawthorne already had his phone out. He knew where the ambulance was headed — and it just so happened that he was on the board of that hospital. So his phone call was immediately put through to the emergency room director, and he started barking orders. "When Chance Valentine comes in, he's to get the best care, you understand? That man will not die. Anything that my daughter wants, anything she needs for his care, you give her immediately. You put your best doctors in there with him and *nothing* can go wrong, do you hear me? *Nothing.* My daughter wants that man healed and—"

"They'll take care of him, Will." Faith's soft voice came from right behind him.

His shoulders stiffened. "I'll be there in fifteen minutes," Will snapped into the phone. "And he'd better already be back in surgery by then." He hung up his phone and turned to face Faith.

Her gun was holstered, her hands folded over her chest and her eyes — *still beautiful enough to break me.*

"You should really learn to ask nicely for things instead of always barking out your orders," she told him. Her voice was mild, but there was sympathy and worry in her eyes.

He stepped closer to her. "You saved Gwen."

"I did my job."

He took another step. "You saved my daughter. *Anything* you want, you have. I know you're up for a promotion, I can make that happen, I can make—"

Her hand lifted and touched his chest. "I was doing my job, and you don't need to make anything happen for me. I do that for myself. Always have. Always will."

Yes, she did. Just one of the many things he admired about her.

"Chance is the one who took the bullets for her, and from what I can gather...he's also the one who shot Daniel Duvato." She pointed to the right, toward the man who'd been strapped in the back of another ambulance, a man under police guard.

Two more ambulances roared up to the scene.

Will kept his gaze on Daniel Duvato. "Will he make it?"

"Maybe. Hard to say at this point. Chance wasn't exactly looking to spare the guy when he pumped his bullets into Daniel."

If Daniel lived and Chance didn't...

"But he won't hurt your daughter again, that's for sure. Because if he does survive, he's going straight to jail."

Another team of EMTs rushed by. This time, they were carrying Devlin Shade on a stretcher. Devlin saw Will and called out, "Chance! Gwen! Are they all right?" His shirt was covered in blood.

"Gwen is," Will yelled back. *I don't know about Chance.*

Devlin blanched. The EMTs secured him in the back of the ambulance.

"So much pain," Will said as his gaze swept the scene. So much...*Why?*

And then he saw the last victim. Ethan Barclay was being wheeled out of Wicked. At first, Will thought the man was dead. Then he saw Ethan's arm moving. Will rushed toward him. "Ethan!"

Ethan's head turned. His eyes were too bright, almost feverish. "M-my fault..." Ethan muttered. "Didn't know...br-brother..."

"What?"

The EMTs forced Will back.

"H-he was…brother…"

The sirens were screaming again.

Will stood there a minute, feeling lost. No, feeling as if he were trapped in hell. Because he remembered another time, another night when violence had torn his world apart. That night, he'd arrived too late. His wife had been gone.

His daughter had stared at him with stark, terror-filled eyes. For weeks after that, Gwen had woken screaming in the night.

Weeks…

Faith touched his shoulder. He flinched away from her.

"You can't control everything," Faith told him, her voice carrying no further than his ears. "You just can't." Her fingers curled around him. This time, he didn't back away.

He'd run from Faith before, because he'd known that she could do so much better than him. A bitter, control freak of a man with too many enemies to count. But, right then…

He pulled her into his arms. Held her tight.

"Thank you," he told her.

Will felt her soft nod.

And he knew he owed Faith, far more than he'd ever be able to repay.

CHAPTER THIRTEEN

Gwen paced in the hospital waiting room. Paced again and again — the same circular path around the little room. As soon as the ambulance had arrived, Chance had been wheeled away. He'd gone to surgery and she'd sunk into her own hell.

She'd watched as the others were brought in — Dev, Ethan, and Daniel. Damn Daniel. Cops had followed him back into surgery and he'd been cuffed to his gurney. She'd seen him, and rage had poured through her. Gwen had lunged toward him, ready to *kill* him right then and there.

But Lex had appeared. He'd pulled her back. He'd wrapped his arms around her and held Gwen until Daniel had disappeared — and until her control had come back.

Lex had told her that Sophie was in the same hospital. She'd been attacked — no doubt, by Daniel, too. Though Gwen didn't understand *why* Daniel had hurt them. It was all still a tangle to her, and she couldn't work out the knots because she was too worried about Chance. She needed Chance. Her steps became faster. More frantic.

How long were the doctors going to take? How long?

The surgery doors swung open. Gwen stopped pacing. She stopped breathing.

The doctor took off his mask. "He's all right. Chance Valentine is in recovery right now. He'll be coming out from the anesthesia soon, and..." The doctor's gaze slipped toward Gwen's father. "He can, um, have one visitor." The doc's stare shifted to Gwen. "Just for a few minutes, ma'am, but you can go back."

She nearly tackled the doctor in her haste to get back there. The scent of the hospital — antiseptic, cleaner — filled her nose as she hurried back to the recovery area. The nurse pointed her toward Chance's area, and then she saw him. Hooked up to so many machines. Looking so pale, lying so still. Her heartbeat stuttered in her chest. "Chance?"

His eyes were closed, but his breathing seemed strong. Deep and even. She inched closer to the bed.

"Chance...the doctor said you are going to be all right."

The machines beeped.

She reached for his hand. For some reason, she'd expected him to be cold to the touch. He wasn't. He was so warm. So very warm. Her Chance.

She bent near the bed and brought his hand to her lips. Gwen kissed his hand. "We're both okay, Chance. It's over. The police have Daniel in custody. We can...we can try for our future now. We can do it." *You just need to get better. Be strong for me.*

The machines beeped. That beeping was reassuring. Constant. Steady.

Gwen kept talking to him. "I should have told you I loved you sooner, right? I knew for a long time. I knew before last Christmas. Why do you think I followed you out onto that balcony? It wasn't just desire, though...yes, you are hot." She smiled. But then the smile vanished as fast as it had appeared. "I've loved you for a long time. I tried to stop, but that didn't really work out for me. I tried to move on, but then I realized...other men weren't you. No one else is quite like you. Stubborn and strong and...so everything that I want. You know me well, Chance, better than anyone else, so I guess part of me always thought...you had to know how I felt. You had to see that I loved you."

She blinked away her tears. Kissed the back of his hand again. "But I don't think you did see it. And I didn't see that you loved me. We were both blind, but we don't have to be anymore. We can go after what we want. We can be happy."

She stared at his face. A face she loved so much. "You just have to get better. You said you'd do anything for me, right? You have to get better. Get stronger. And give me the life that I want. Give me a life with you. Because I won't take anything else."

She kept talking to him. Promising him a Christmas together. Promising that they'd get a tree. That in the summer, they'd take a trip. Maybe go to some exotic island and spend the days naked together on some beautiful beach. "We can do anything," Gwen told him. "As long as we're together. Any dream we want, we can have." She swallowed. A thick lump wanted to fill her throat. "I just need you. I need you to open your eyes. To be with me."

A soft knock came from behind her.

"Miss…"

Gwen looked over her shoulder. A nurse stood there.

"I'm sorry," the woman told her softly, "but your time is up. You'll be able to visit with the patient again later, I promise."

Gwen rose. Her hand still held his. She turned away, her fingers beginning to slide away from Chance's hand.

His fingers tightened around hers.

Gwen's breath caught. Her gaze immediately flew to Chance's face. His eyelids were opening.

"Any…thing…" Chance managed, his voice rasping. "Told you…anything…for you…"

She shot back toward that bed. Kissed him. Ignored the wires and beeping and everything else.

"Never l-leave you…" Chance whispered. "Always…my Gwen…"

She kissed him again. She tasted her own tears. And she tasted happiness.

A life together. That was what they'd have. A future.

Love.

***

Five days later…

"You know you shouldn't be here," Faith murmured to Chance. "You just got out of the hospital."

"I'm fine." Well, actually, he was fucking pissed. He stared through the one-way mirror, his gaze locked on the face of Daniel Duvato. Daniel had gotten out of the hospital the day before, too. The guy was pale and currently handcuffed as he sat at the small table in the interrogation room.

Daniel wasn't alone. Ethan Barclay stood across from him.

Daniel hadn't asked for a lawyer. He'd just asked to speak with Ethan.

"They're brothers," Faith said.

They didn't look like brothers. The two men appeared to be nothing alike.

"At least, that's what we pieced together," Faith continued as she cocked her head and studied the two men. "Seems Ethan's father stepped out on Ethan and his mom. The guy got a young waitress named Donna Duvato pregnant. He kept her on the side for years...but he let it be clear to little Daniel that the boy wasn't part of his *real* family."

Right. Because that kind of shit didn't screw with a person's mind.

"From all accounts, Hank Barclay was one straight asshole." Faith's voice had hardened. Her arm brushed Chance's as she stepped closer to the glass. "The guy abused Ethan and his mother for years. Daniel had no idea just how twisted the bastard could be."

Chance wasn't so sure of that. "Maybe Daniel was just more like dear old dad than Ethan was."

Faith glanced at him, surprise flashing on her face. "Maybe." She nodded as she seemed to consider this. "Maybe he was..."

Then Ethan started talking.

***

"You killed Jena Parker," Ethan said as he stared into Daniel's eyes. Daniel Duvato. The man had been working for him...*for years*. Daniel had been his driver, his body guard, the bouncer at his club...Ethan had trusted the guy implicitly, and Daniel had been working to destroy him all along.

Daniel laughed. "Do you remember when she accused you of cheating on her? See...I'm the one who told her you did that. I thought she'd dump your ass for good, but the dumb bitch just took your sorry self right back. She was even still planning to marry you."

Dumb bitch. Ethan's hands clenched into fists. His stitches pulled. He had so many stitches now, thanks to this asshole. More than he could count. *He turned me into a monster.*

"So yeah, I played with her brakes." Daniel shrugged. "Not my fault she drove too fast, though...that was all on her."

Sonofabitch.

"And Marjorie?" Ethan forced himself to ask. "You killed her, too?" The detective — Faith Chestang — had told him to get a confession from Daniel. If the bastard wanted to talk, if he wanted to dig his own grave, then Ethan was supposed to let him.

Daniel's laughter came again. "She never even saw me coming." He shook his head. "I'd heard you and Sophie talking about her. I knew where she'd went. I just had to bide my time and wait…wait for just the right moment to slip away and go after Marjorie."

Sophie. The pain was there, knifing through him. This bastard had gone after her, too.

"You had a partner," Ethan said this with quiet rage. "Someone was helping you all along. There's no way you did this on your own—"

"Why? You think I'm not *smart* enough to pull this off? You think you're the only one with brains?" Hate hardened Daniel's face. "This was all my plan. Sure, I got my buddy Carl to drive the van for me, paid him a few hundred, but that was just so I would have a ride waiting. Because I was too clever to get caught at Gwen's place. Everything else…*all fucking me.*"

And there was the last of his confession. All tied up in a neat bow. Did the guy even realize he'd just sent himself to prison? Did he even care? Or was he really that fucked up in the head?

"Sorry about Sophie," Daniel said suddenly. He actually sounded like he meant those words. "I liked her, but, after that last car ride, I realized she had to go. You'd always be happy, as long as she was there. Always have a family…with Sophie. So I killed her."

This time, Ethan shook his head. "Sophie isn't dead."

Daniel's face went slack with surprise.

"She's not dead. She was in the same hospital you were. She recovered fully." He crept closer to the table. The rage inside of him was bubbling up. He'd gotten the confession. Now...*I want to know why.* "You're my brother."

A brother he hadn't known about. Not until he'd gone into Wicked five days ago, and Daniel had attacked him. The bastard had been screaming about how unfair life was...how Ethan needed to see what it was like to have no one, *nothing.*

"He fucked my mother." Daniel's voice shook with his own fury. "Then he treated us like shit for the next fifteen years. We lived in poverty. We had *nothing.* And he'd come over, he'd screw her, then go back to the perfect life he had with you."

Ethan stalked closer to his brother. "You're so damn clueless."

Daniel glared at him. "I'm not the one who didn't see me...right there, all those years. You didn't know, you didn't—"

"*You* were the lucky one. He came home to us all right. Only to beat the hell out of my mom. She was his punching bag. So was I. I was the one he hit again and again and—" Ethan glanced toward the glass. "Turn off the recording!" he yelled. "Nothing else is on record! I'm done."

He waited, knowing Faith would do as he'd asked. After all, he'd stepped into hell to get this confession for her.

He waited…

Then he grabbed his brother's head and slammed it into the table. He figured he'd have less than a minute before the cops had to come in.

"He hit us again and again," Ethan whispered into Daniel's ear. "Until I stopped him. Until I fought back and I killed the bastard. I made him suffer before he died. Just as he'd made me suffer."

He put his hands around Daniel's throat. Tightened them. Daniel started to gasp.

"If you ever come after me again, I'll do the same to you," he promised. "So you'd better pray they never let you out of jail…because if they do…*brother*," Ethan spat, "*you're as dead as our father.*"

The doors flew open. Faith stood there, glaring at him. "Let the perp go!"

Daniel was struggling to breathe, and Ethan wasn't letting him go.

Faith shook her head. "You know he's not worth it."

"I've got friends in prison," Ethan muttered into Daniel's ear. "Maybe you won't survive very long…" Then he let Daniel go. He sucked in a deep breath. Straightened his shoulders.

Ethan headed toward Faith. She glanced down at his shirt. "You must have popped some of your stitches," she said, voice expressionless. "You're bleeding."

The pain had been worth it. He passed by her and found Chance standing in the hallway. The interrogation room door shut behind Ethan, and the two men measured each other.

"I'm sorry," Ethan finally said. "For everything that happened to Gwen. I never wanted her hurt."

Chance nodded. "I know."

Ethan swallowed. "You love her."

Again, Chance nodded.

"Gwen deserves to be happy. Treat her well." He kept his spine straight as he strode forward.

Chance stepped in his path.

Hell.

He waited for the punch that had to be coming.

But Chance said, "Don't let what that bastard did...don't let it destroy you. We can all be more than our pasts. So much more." Then Chance turned around and left.

Ethan's shoulders sagged. *I want to be more*...But, some days, he just wasn't sure if he could be.

***

The snow was falling again. Chance stood outside of Gwen's apartment, the snowflakes drifting down on him, and he thought about the twists and turns a life could take.

When he'd been in the hospital, Gwen had stayed by his side. Every moment. And every time he'd looked into her eyes, he'd realized just how damn lucky he was.

Gwen loved him. Truly loved him. She knew he wasn't perfect. She knew he had a darkness inside. Knew just what he was capable of doing.

And she still loved him.

I am such a lucky bastard. Because he didn't deserve her. Not really.

But he'd be damned if he ever let her go.

After he'd listened to that interrogation at the police station, he'd been more determined than ever to spend the rest of his life with Gwen. She was all that he wanted. And he'd move heaven and earth to make her happy. Hell, he'd deal with the devil if it meant Gwen would always be safe.

He headed toward her building. It was time to stop watching. Time to take the next step. He rode the elevator up to her apartment. Knocked on her door. The snowflakes had melted on his coat when she opened that door.

And he was down on his knees.

"Chance?"

He took the ring box out of his pocket. He opened it. Chance stared up at Gwen, knowing this was the most important moment of his life.

"I love you," he told her simply. Because there really wasn't anything else to say. "Will you marry me, Gwen?"

She smiled. A slow, beautiful smile that lit her eyes, that lit her whole face. Gwen nodded. She pulled him to his feet, then she pulled Chance into her apartment.

There weren't cameras hidden there any longer. No one to watch them.

Just us.

He shut the door behind him. Pulled Gwen even closer. He slid the ring onto her finger. A perfect fit, just like she was to him.

Perfect.

Chance kissed her and knew that his life had just altered. He wasn't going to desperately dream any more, wasn't going to wake, reaching for Gwen...only to find that she wasn't there.

Now, she'd be with him. He'd be with her.

Always.

And if anyone ever tried to hurt her again...

He'd fucking destroy them. Because Gwen was the woman he'd fight to protect. The woman he'd die to possess...the woman who'd brought him to his knees.

His world. His life.

His.

###

Coming in January of 2015…
WANT ME (Lex & Sophie's book)

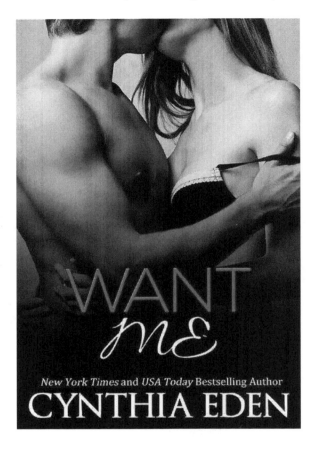

New York Times and USA Today Bestselling Author
CYNTHIA EDEN

A NOTE FROM THE AUTHOR

Thank you so much for reading Watch Me! This book is the first in my new "Dark Obsession" series—the next book, WANT ME, will be available in January of 2015.

If you'd like to stay updated on all of my book releases and sales, please join my newsletter list www.cynthiaeden.com/newsletter/. You can also check out my Facebook page www.facebook.com/cynthiaedenfanpage. I love to post giveaways over at Facebook—so be sure to check in for your chance to win!

Again, thank you for reading Watch Me.

Best,

Cynthia Eden

www.cynthiaeden.com

ABOUT THE AUTHOR

Award-winning author Cynthia Eden writes dark tales of paranormal romance and romantic suspense. She is a *New York Times, USA Today, Digital Book World,* and *IndieReader* bestseller. Cynthia is also a two-time finalist for the RITA® award (she was a finalist both in the romantic suspense category and in the paranormal romance category). Since she began writing full-time in 2005, Cynthia has written over fifty novels and novellas.

Cynthia is a southern girl who loves horror movies, chocolate, and happy endings. More information about Cynthia and her books may be found at: http://www.cynthiaeden.com or on her Facebook page at: http://www.facebook.com/cynthiaedenfanpage. Cynthia is also on Twitter at http://www.twitter.com/cynthiaeden.

HER WORKS

List of Cynthia Eden's romantic suspense titles:

- MINE TO TAKE (Mine, Book 1)
- MINE TO KEEP (Mine, Book 2)
- MINE TO HOLD (Mine, Book 3)
- MINE TO CRAVE (Mine, Book 4)
- MINE TO HAVE (Mine, Book 5)
- FIRST TASTE OF DARKNESS
- SINFUL SECRETS
- DIE FOR ME (For Me, Book 1)
- FEAR FOR ME (For Me, Book 2)
- SCREAM FOR ME (For Me, Book 3)
- DEADLY FEAR (Deadly, Book 1)
- DEADLY HEAT (Deadly, Book 2)
- DEADLY LIES (Deadly, Book 3)
- ALPHA ONE (Shadow Agents, Book 1)
- GUARDIAN RANGER (Shadow Agents, Book 2)
- SHARPSHOOTER (Shadow Agents, Book 3)
- GLITTER AND GUNFIRE (Shadow Agents, Book 4)

- UNDERCOVER CAPTOR (Shadow Agents, Book 5)
- THE GIRL NEXT DOOR (Shadow Agents, Book 6)
- EVIDENCE OF PASSION (Shadow Agents, Book 7)
- WAY OF THE SHADOWS (Shadow Agents, Book 8)

Paranormal romances by Cynthia Eden:
- BOUND BY BLOOD (Bound, Book 1)
- BOUND IN DARKNESS (Bound, Book 2)
- BOUND IN SIN (Bound, Book 3)
- BOUND BY THE NIGHT (Bound, Book 4)
- *FOREVER BOUND - An anthology containing: BOUND BY BLOOD, BOUND IN DARKNESS, BOUND IN SIN, AND BOUND BY THE NIGHT
- BOUND IN DEATH (Bound, Book 5)
- THE WOLF WITHIN (Purgatory, Book 1)
- MARKED BY THE VAMPIRE (Purgatory, Book 2)
- CHARMING THE BEAST (Purgatory, Book 3)

Other paranormal romances by Cynthia Eden:
- A VAMPIRE'S CHRISTMAS CAROL
- BLEED FOR ME
- BURN FOR ME (Phoenix Fire, Book 1)

- ONCE BITTEN, TWICE BURNED (Phoenix Fire, Book 2)
- PLAYING WITH FIRE (Phoenix Fire, Book 3)
- ANGEL OF DARKNESS (Fallen, Book 1)
- ANGEL BETRAYED (Fallen, Book 2)
- ANGEL IN CHAINS (Fallen, Book 3)
- AVENGING ANGEL (Fallen, Book 4)
- IMMORTAL DANGER
- NEVER CRY WOLF
- A BIT OF BITE (Free Read!!)
- ETERNAL HUNTER (Night Watch, Book 1)
- I'LL BE SLAYING YOU (Night Watch, Book 2)
- ETERNAL FLAME (Night Watch, Book 3)
- HOTTER AFTER MIDNIGHT (Midnight, Book 1)
- MIDNIGHT SINS (Midnight, Book 2)
- MIDNIGHT'S MASTER (Midnight, Book 3)
- WHEN HE WAS BAD (anthology)
- EVERLASTING BAD BOYS (anthology)
- BELONG TO THE NIGHT (anthology)

Made in the USA
Lexington, KY
02 February 2015